Hannah
On Her Way

Hannah
On Her Way

CLAUDIA
MILLS

MACMILLAN PUBLISHING COMPANY
New York

COLLIER MACMILLAN CANADA
Toronto

MAXWELL MACMILLAN INTERNATIONAL PUBLISHING GROUP
New York · *Oxford* · *Singapore* · *Sydney*

Macmillan Publishing Company
866 Third Avenue
New York, NY 10022
Collier Macmillan Canada, Inc.
1200 Eglinton Avenue East
Suite 200
Don Mills, Ontario M3C 3N1
First edition
Printed in the United States of America

10 9 8 7 6 5 4 3 2 1

Library of Congress Cataloging-in-Publication Data

Mills, Claudia.
Hannah on her way / Claudia Mills. — 1st ed.
p.   cm.
Summary: Quiet, introspective Hannah Keddie is surprised when she is befriended by the
other new girl at school, popular Caitie Crystal.
ISBN 0-02-767011-2
[1. Friendship—Fiction.   2.Popularity—Fiction.   3. Schools—Fiction.]   I. Title.
PZ7.M63963Han   1991   [Fic]—dc20
90-46532

The text of this book is set in 12 1/2 point Garamond
Designed by REM Studio, Inc.

For Beverly Reingold,
editor and friend,
with thanks and love

—————————————

Hannah
On Her Way

1

Hannah Keddie didn't need to leave her snug cocoon of patchwork quilts to know that it was snowing outside, hard, and that there would be no school that day. It was the silence of the snow that awakened her. It was always quiet out in the country where the Keddies lived, but the snow made a different kind of stillness, a hush that settled around their old farmhouse like an enchantment. A pale light filled her room, the diffuse glow of the yard lights reflected by the whiteness of snow, snow everywhere.

Hannah looked at the clock by her bed. Five-thirty. Careful not to wake her doll Judith, sleeping next to her, she slipped out of bed, thrust her feet into her sock-slippers, wrapped her robe around her, and tiptoed downstairs to the kitchen.

Her father was there before her, already dressed, building up the fire in the wood-burning stove. He nodded to Hannah, but didn't speak. The Keddies were all early risers, but they didn't believe in conversations before breakfast. Dawn was the time for work, for solitude, for one's own private, quiet thoughts.

Hannah reached for the box of colored pencils and the sketch pad she had left on the kitchen table the night before. For Hannah, early morning was the time to draw. But she was too happy to start working right away. *No school, no school, no school!* She must have dreaded school more than she realized. The thought of its cancellation lifted a weight from her heart that she had hardly realized was there.

She curled up in the big rocking chair in the corner of the kitchen and watched her father. Paul Keddie hummed as he piled log upon log and poked the sleepy embers into flame. Although Hannah had felt like humming and singing and shouting a moment ago, she no longer did. Much as she tried to hold on to the glorious feeling of snow-day freedom, she found herself thinking about school.

School. She didn't hate it, exactly; she just wished she never had to go there again. Hannah was good at school and liked most of her subjects, except, of course, gym. No, schoolwork itself wasn't the problem. And it didn't bother Hannah that school had little to do with anything that really mattered to her, like art or books (real books you read just because you wanted to) or being outdoors on a misty morning before anyone else in the world was awake.

The real problem with school was friends, or,

rather, her lack of them. The Keddies had moved often, as Hannah's father had gone from one postdoctoral research appointment to another. Hannah had gone to four different schools since kindergarten. It was hard making friends when you were always the new girl. And even though Hannah had been at Greenwood Park Elementary School now since September, the other fifth-grade girls there were different. All they ever talked about was clothes and boys and makeup.

Hannah thought that was silly, and besides, she wasn't, well, *ready* yet. She was only ten years old! Not sixteen, or twenty, or twenty-five. She knew Dawn Klein, the ringleader of the popular girls, thought she was babyish. Dawn's new best friend, Caitie Crystal, probably thought so, too. Fine! Hannah didn't want to be friends with girls like Dawn and Caitie, not if it meant she had to grow up overnight and try to care about the things they cared about. Anyway, she didn't really need friends: She had her family, and her artwork, and a whole library full of books left to read. And yet . . .

Hannah drew back the curtain. A neat little loaf of snow, six inches high, sat on top of the bird feeder, and the snow was still falling, enormous flakes like limp white doilies.

"What's the matter, Hannikin?" her father asked, standing up and brushing bits of snowy bark from his rough wool jacket.

"Nothing." The question, breaking the early morning silence, surprised her. "Why?"

"I don't know," he said. "You looked so sad there for a minute."

"I was just thinking," Hannah said. She wasn't sad about school. Not really *sad*.

Hannah sketched until breakfast—quick impressions of their huge orange cat, Hildegarde: Hildegarde snoozing by the stove; Hildegarde silhouetted against the window, gazing out at the snow. The painter Andrew Wyeth had made dozens of portraits of a woman named Helga. Hannah's parents had taken her to see the Helga paintings at the National Gallery of Art in Washington. These would be Hannah's Hildegarde paintings.

Hannah's mother appeared in the kitchen as her husband began frying sausages and potatoes and chunks of tart Granny Smith apples all together in his cast-iron skillet. She had a smudge of gray clay on her nose and another streak of clay across her forehead. Susan Keddie was a potter. The damp, earthy smell of clay clung to her like a perfume.

"It's official," she announced. "I heard the school closings on the radio in my studio. Montgomery County schools are closed, and classes at the University of Maryland are cancelled!"

Hannah's father waved his spatula in jubilation.

After all the family's moves, he had settled down this year to a long-term job teaching in the astronomy department at the university's College Park campus. "Let it snow! Let it snow! Let it snow!" he sang.

Hannah's mother ran a finger down the length of Hannah's long blond braid. "It's supposed to stop by ten or so. We'll make snow sculptures this afternoon. It's good wet snow, perfect for packing."

With the sausage and potatoes and apples, Hannah's father served cinnamon toast, as well—thick slices of golden toast dripping with butter and cinnamon sugar. Hannah's father believed in special feasts for special occasions, like snow-day mornings. In a way it would have made more sense to have a breakfast feast on a regular school day and just munch cold cereal on holidays. Why should all the wonderful things be bunched together: no school *and* snow sculptures *and* home fried potatoes with cinnamon toast?

After breakfast, Hannah washed the dishes and then went upstairs to work on a book report on this week's favorite book, *The Princess and the Goblin.* But first she got Judith up out of bed, brushed her hair, and sat her by the window so she could see the snow. Dorothy had toppled off the bureau, so Hannah picked her up, comforted her, and set her down next to Judith. Not that she *seemed* to need much comforting. Dolls couldn't talk or cry or change the expressions on their sweet painted faces. But that didn't mean they didn't have feelings. Hannah didn't show anyone at Greenwood Park that she had feelings, but she did.

The Keddies had never made more magnificent snow sculptures. They all agreed: This time they had outdone themselves. Hannah's father created a medieval castle, complete with moat and drawbridge and crenellated towers. Hannah's mother made an enormous Easter basket, with a bunny rabbit inside. Hannah decided on the duckling family from *Make Way for Ducklings.* By the time they finished, the sky was pink above the snow, pinkish pearl shot through with streaks of crimson.

Hannah's mother had made chili in the crockpot, so supper was waiting for them when they trooped in, frozen and ravenous. It was as if Goldilocks had left a nice steaming hot supper for the three bears to enjoy when they returned at the end of the day to their cottage in the woods.

Hannah suddenly gave her mother a tight, squeezing hug. It was hard for her to believe that other children loved their parents as much as she loved hers.

"It's a shame that more people don't drive by this way," her father said, halfway through his first bowl of chili. "We could put up a sign for our snow sculptures, charge admission—"

"No!" Hannah and her mother said together.

"The best things in life are free and all that?"

"Snow is, at least," her mother said firmly.

"But you know what I wish?" Hannah asked. "I wish they would never melt. I mean, we worked so hard to make them, and they're the best ones we ever did. I wish we could find a way to keep them frozen forever, just like they are today."

"No!" This time it was her parents who were united in disagreement.

"That's part of the magic of snow sculptures," Hannah's mother explained. "They're *not* permanent. They're not meant to be. They come with the snow and disappear with the sun."

"Here today, gone tomorrow," her father chimed in cheerfully. "And who knows? Tomorrow may bring something even better."

But Hannah knew it wouldn't. Today had brought snow. Tomorrow would bring school.

2

The next day was bitter cold, for Maryland, with the temperature at dawn just above zero. But most of the major roads had been plowed, and school was open.

A test in science, the mid-Atlantic states in social studies, and it was time for art, Hannah's biggest disappointment now that Mrs. Kaplan, the regular art teacher, was out for the rest of the year on maternity leave.

Hannah groaned to herself as Mrs. McCloskey, the substitute art teacher, began explaining the week's new project. On the teacher's desk in front of the room sat a sample piggy bank made out of an empty plastic Clorox bottle. Laid on its side, the bottle did have a vaguely piglike shape. A small circle of pink felt, dotted with two Magic Marker nostrils, was glued to the bottle cap to make a snout. Four corks served as feet, and a curly pink pipe cleaner pierced the hind end for a tail. The pig's big white body was decorated with flower shapes cut from scraps of felt.

"And then," Mrs. McCloskey said, scissors in hand, "you'll cut a little slot—not too big!—in the top of your piggy to turn him into a bank. See?"

Sitting next to Hannah, Caitie Crystal yawned and put her head down on her desk.

"Caitlin, are you watching?" Mrs. McCloskey asked.

"Yes," Caitie said. She raised her head half an inch, but as soon as Mrs. McCloskey looked away, she buried it again in her folded arms.

Caitie was new at Greenwood Park, newer even than Hannah, but in a few short weeks she had already become Dawn's best friend—and the despair of the fifth-grade teachers. Caitie's projects were always the worst and sloppiest in the class.

Hannah's projects were always the neatest and the best, but she didn't know if she could stand making one more thing out of one more Clorox bottle. Last week they had made vases, covering the Clorox bottles with wrapped twine. The week before they had cut the Clorox bottles in half to make planters. Since Mrs. McCloskey had arrived, right before Christmas, she had assigned six Clorox bottle projects. There must be a book full of them: *101 Uses for Empty Clorox Bottles.* Six down, ninety-five to go. Where did she get all the bottles? Hannah wanted to know. How many Clorox bottles could there be in the world?

"Where does she keep them?" Caitie hissed across the aisle.

At first Hannah didn't realize Caitie was talking to her. "Keep what?"

But there could be only one answer. "Her whole house must be Clorox bottles," Caitie said, more loudly. "What do you bet she has a Clorox bottle couch and Clorox bottle chairs and a Clorox bottle coffee table and—"

"Caitlin," Mrs. McCloskey called out. "Let's not have any talking."

Caitie's head went down again.

"Hannah? Would you help me hand out the Clorox bottles?"

Dutifully, Hannah began setting a Clorox bottle on each desk. But she wished she were handing out tubes of oil paints, or boxes of pastel chalks, or bottles of india ink, or sticks of soft, smudgy charcoal. If only Greenwood Park had gotten a real art teacher instead of an expert in the many uses of the Clorox bottle. With Mrs. Kaplan, Hannah had actually loved school for forty-five whole minutes every week.

There were twenty-five kids in the class, but, Hannah found out, only twenty-three Clorox bottles in Mrs. McCloskey's huge cardboard carton.

"I need two more," she told the teacher. "For Caitie and me."

Mrs. McCloskey clucked in exasperation. "I'll

have to go to my car and get them." Aha! Hannah and Caitie exchanged glances. "You two can start cutting out your felt flowers while I'm gone." She bustled out of the room, looking with her stout figure not unlike a Clorox bottle herself.

"Do you have any nail polish remover?" Caitie asked Hannah even before Mrs. McCloskey had closed the door behind her.

Hannah shook her head. Wasn't the answer obvious? Hannah didn't own a bottle of nail polish remover, or of nail polish, either. She had never worn nail polish in her life, or makeup, or, for that matter, clothes like Caitie's and Dawn's—stylish grown-up clothes that made them look like the girls Hannah saw walking home from the high school.

"I do," Dawn called out from two rows back. She passed the small bottle up to Caitie. Caitie and Dawn had sat next to each other until Mrs. Harding, their regular fifth-grade teacher, had separated them last Friday to keep Caitie from talking. She must have figured that a seat next to Hannah was safe.

"Do you have a cotton ball?" Caitie asked Hannah. Keeping Caitie from talking was obviously going to be harder than Mrs. Harding realized.

Hannah shook her head again.

"A Kleenex?"

That Hannah had. She handed one across the aisle, then watched, fascinated in spite of herself, as

Caitie moistened the tissue with nail polish remover and began systematically wiping bright pink nail polish off each fingernail.

Hannah knew she should be cutting out her felt flowers. But instead of reaching for her scissors, she took her sketch pad and a box of worn colored pencils out of her desk. With a few quick strokes she drew in the shape of Caitie's head—her short smooth cap of hair, the tilt of her nose. Then she drew Caitie's mouth, pink with lipstick, and the collar of her blouse.

"What are you drawing?" Caitie leaned over to look. "Is it me? It *is* me! Where did you learn to draw like that? Can I have it when it's done?"

Caitie's excitement made Hannah feel shy and self-conscious. "It's just a sketch." But she knew it was good. She began adding some shadows and contours to Caitie's face.

Absorbed in her sketch, Hannah didn't hear Mrs. McCloskey return. Suddenly a Clorox bottle was plunked down in front of her, hard.

"Hannah, Caitie, I thought I told you to get to work. I'm disappointed in both of you."

Flushing, Hannah started to put her sketch away. It was the best one she had ever done.

"Hannah *is* working," Caitie said. "Let her finish."

"I'm sorry, Caitlin, but this is art class," Mrs. McCloskey said stiffly. "In art class, you're supposed to be working on *art.*"

"Hannah's picture *is* art. Real art. Not like a dumb old Clorox bottle."

Hannah's heart stopped. Caitie should have known better. Mrs. McCloskey loved dumb old Clorox bottles. She could hardly be expected to ignore such an insult to them.

Sure enough, two spots of red burned in the teacher's plump cheeks. "And your *manicure,* Caitlin? That is real art, too, I suppose? Both of you, go to Mr. Blake's office. You can work on your *real* art projects there."

"Thank you," Caitie said. "Come on, Hannah, let's go."

Numbly, Hannah gathered up her sketch pad and pencils and slipped them back into her desk. She had never been sent to the principal's office, not once in all her years at all those different schools. Why couldn't Caitie have kept her mouth shut? Caitie might not care about doing well in school, but Hannah did.

And yet the Clorox bottles *were* dumb. Caitie hadn't said anything that wasn't true. Maybe now Mrs. McCloskey wouldn't assign another Clorox bottle project for a few weeks. Or even for the rest of the year.

While the others stared, Hannah followed Caitie out of the room. She was furious with Caitie, she really was. Still, an odd tingle of excitement stole over her. She had a feeling, just a feeling, that a lot of things were going to be different now that she sat next to Caitie Crystal.

3

"Free at last," Caitie said, once they were out in the hall. "Where should we go?"

Hannah didn't have to pretend to be shocked. "To the *office*. We have to. You know we do."

"Just kidding," Caitie said. She stopped at the drinking fountain for a long, luxurious drink. "My cousin Bonnie's in high school. There when you get kicked out of class, you go across the street to the Dunkin' Donuts and get donut holes and diet Cokes."

"Don't they get in trouble? I mean, in even worse trouble?"

"If they get caught they do. Bonnie got suspended once."

Really, the Crystals sounded practically like *criminals*. It began to sink in to Hannah that she, Hannah Marie Keddie, had herself been kicked out of class. *Kicked out of class.* It sounded terrible. And it was all Caitie's fault.

Caitie stopped again to check her reflection in the glass of the display case outside the main office. She shook her head to make her silver earrings swing back and forth. "Do you think I should get a second set of holes pierced?"

"Hurry *up,* Caitie!"

"Where's the fire?" But Caitie joined Hannah at the office door.

Mrs. Chan, the school secretary, looked up from her typewriter when the girls entered. "Caitie Crystal," she said with a sigh. "What is it this time, Caitlin?"

"Oh, it's terrible, all right: Mrs. McCloskey got upset because Hannah was working on an art project during art class."

Mrs. Chan looked confused. "Hannah? I never expected to have to write up a discipline form for *you.*"

"Me, either," Hannah said miserably. "It was just, well, Mrs. McCloskey didn't like the things we were working on, and I guess we were fresh to her about them." She was getting madder at Caitie by the minute.

"Well, take a seat. Mr. Blake isn't here right now, but I'll make sure he sees your discipline forms when he returns."

Caitie uncapped her bottle of nail polish remover and busily started in on her left hand as if the outer office were her own private beauty parlor.

"Put that away, Caitlin."

"Mrs. McCloskey said we could work on our projects here," Caitie protested innocently. "She distinctly said, 'Go to Mr. Blake's office. You can work on your projects there.' Didn't she, Hannah?"

"That's enough, Caitie. I mean it."

Caitie put the bottle away, and Hannah turned to gaze at the bulletin board. JANUARY FUN AT GREENWOOD PARK! the construction paper letters read. But today was turning out to be anything but fun for Hannah.

Would this half hour ever *end*? Sitting in the glass-walled office, in full view of any passersby, was like sitting in the stocks at Williamsburg or Old Sturbridge Village. The worst of the punishment was having people *look* at you and know you were being punished. When Mrs. Tomacki, the school librarian, came into the office, she started to smile at Hannah: Mrs. Tomacki was the best friend Hannah had made so far in Maryland. But Hannah flushed so deeply with shame that Mrs. Tomacki's smile died on her lips, and the librarian turned away, looking worried.

If the period ever ended, Hannah vowed, she would never get into trouble again. If she had to do a thousand Clorox-bottle projects, all in a row, she'd do them, one after the other, without complaining.

The bell rang. "Okay, girls, you may go."

Free at last! This time it was true.

Out in the hall again, Caitie grabbed Hannah's arm. "Talk about a big nothing," she said. "But what else can they do? It's against the law to hit you, and they can't take away TV because in school there isn't any. Do you want to have lunch with me and Dawn? You can finish your picture."

Hannah didn't say anything. She didn't trust herself to speak.

Caitie looked at her, puzzled. "Listen, you're not mad, are you, that I got you into trouble? You didn't want to stay in McCloskey's boring class, did you?"

"No, but—I mean, yes, I did. Now Mrs. McCloskey hates me, and Mrs. Chan thinks I'm a troublemaker, and you saw how Mrs. Tomacki looked at me."

"They'll get over it. Don't be mad. What did I say that was so terrible, anyway?"

"You said her Clorox bottles were dumb," Hannah repeated coldly. But as the words came out, she found her mouth beginning to twitch into a grin.

"Well, and aren't they? Answer me that. And wasn't that pig today the dumbest one yet?"

"I don't know," Hannah said, trying to be fair. "The planter was pretty dumb, too."

Suddenly both girls were shrieking with laughter, clutching each other so they wouldn't fall in a heap on the white linoleum, laughing till Hannah's eyes streamed and her stomach ached.

"Girls!" Mrs. Chan stuck her head out of the office. "People are trying to work in here."

The scolding only set off a second tidal wave of

laughter, but Hannah and Caitie made themselves start down the hall. Other kids, on the way to lunch, stared.

"So eat with us," Caitie said, once she had stopped laughing enough to speak.

Hannah wiped her eyes. "I work in the library during lunch," she said. Lunch every day in the school library: Caitie would think she was a baby now, for sure. Not that Hannah really cared what Caitie Crystal thought about anything.

"Then come over after school, okay?"

Hannah hesitated. She had homework to do and her Hildegarde paintings to work on. Still, it was hard to resist Caitie's aggressive friendliness.

"I don't live very far. By the park. Our house-keeper will drive you home."

No. It was impossible, utterly impossible, that she and Caitie Crystal, of all people, would be friends.

"I can't," Hannah said. "I'm sorry, but I just . . . can't."

Then Caitie was gone, and Hannah turned her footsteps to the library, not knowing if she felt relieved at having turned down Caitie's invitation, or sorry.

4

Greenwood Park Elementary School had a wonderful library—large and spacious, with windows looking out on the snowy lawn. There were lots of low, inviting tables and a couch just right for curling up in with a lapful of books. Mrs. Tomacki was a librarian worthy of such a library. Hannah suspected that Mrs. Tomacki had read every book on every shelf in every section. She could never discover a book that Mrs. Tomacki hadn't already read, weeks or months or years ahead of her.

Hannah's lunch sessions in the library had begun as a weekly book discussion group back in September, when she had first arrived at Greenwood Park. Seven or eight fifth graders had met in the library at lunchtime to discuss a different book every week. But gradually the other kids had drifted away, leaving only Hannah and Mrs. Tomacki. Mrs. Tomacki must have guessed what the book group sessions meant to Hannah, because she invited Hannah to bring her lunch to the library as often as she liked, which had turned out to be just about every day. Sometimes Hannah shelved books or pasted library cards in the back of new books or made posters for special library events. Other times she studied, or she and Mrs. Tomacki just talked, about books, about art, about everything.

That day Mrs. Tomacki raised a quizzical eyebrow when Hannah slipped in.

Hannah supplied the question for her: "What was I doing in the office with Caitie? Well, it's kind of a long story."

"I love stories," Mrs. Tomacki said.

So Hannah told her. Mrs. Tomacki laughed when Hannah reached the part about Caitie's Clorox bottle rebellion, but when Hannah finished, she turned serious again.

"I know it's hard not to have a real art teacher to work with now that Mrs. Kaplan's gone. But I think Mrs. McCloskey is doing her best. Her background isn't in art, you know. And it's a challenge keeping the interest of bright kids like you and Caitie."

Hannah felt a stab of remorse for laughing at the Clorox bottles. She wasn't sure she wanted to be compared with bored, lazy Caitie Crystal, either.

"You're going to have to think about some other avenues for your art, Hannah," Mrs. Tomacki said. "Has Mrs. McCloskey talked to your class about the superintendent of schools' countywide art contest?"

Hannah shook her head.

"Any student in the county can enter, to be judged against other students at his or her own grade level. The choice of subject is up to each individual artist, as is the choice of artistic medium."

Hannah twirled the end of her braid around her index finger. She knew what Mrs. Tomacki was going to say next.

"I think you should enter that contest, Hannah. It would give you something to work toward this spring. I'd be happy to look over whatever you feel are your strongest pieces and help you decide which one to submit. What do you say? Should we give it our best try?"

"I don't want to," Hannah said, surprised at how stubborn she sounded. But she hated contests. Once, when she was in third grade, she had secretly mailed in a picture to an art contest in one of the children's magazines. It was just a picture of a tree, but at the time she had thought it was a beautiful picture of a beautiful tree and surely better than most third graders could do. She had been so excited, counting the days till the May issue of the magazine would appear, announcing the prizes. When it finally arrived in the mail, she had torn off the brown-paper wrapper and turned with trembling fingers to the children's page. But her picture wasn't there.

She still remembered the shock of disbelief at not seeing it. Could she have missed it somehow? But no matter how hard she stared at the page, her picture still wasn't there. Worse, the pictures that *were* there were terrible—little grinning stick figures like a kindergartner would draw. Her picture hadn't even been picked as better than those.

"I don't believe in contests," Hannah said now. "I think they're dumb."

Mrs. Tomacki looked mildly taken aback, but all she said was, "You don't have to decide until spring. But I want you at least to think about it."

"Okay," Hannah said. There was no harm in *thinking.*

"Now, tell me what you've been reading," Mrs. Tomacki said. "Anything wonderful?"

"The Princess and the Goblin," Hannah answered promptly, relieved at the change in subject. Contests really *were* dumb, especially when you knew you wouldn't win.

All afternoon Caitie whispered to Hannah across the aisle between their desks. Could she have another tissue? Did Hannah have an extra pencil? What page were they supposed to turn to in their language arts books? Hannah handed Caitie the supplies she wanted, but tried her best not to engage in any real conversations. Caitie had gotten her into enough trouble for one day. All Hannah needed now was to be sent to the office for talking. When the closing bell finally rang, she hurried out to the bus line, glad to be going home alone.

However, the next day Caitie chattered away again throughout the morning, and when the girls lined up for gym, Hannah found Caitie next to her, still talking.

"Hooray, hooray, we're starting gymnastics today," Caitie informed her. "I saw them setting up the equipment this morning."

Hannah's heart sank. Sure enough, across the gym she recognized the parallel bars and the long leather horse and the horrid little buck, like a short squat horse without any handles. She had never had gymnastics in any of her other schools, but she had tried taking a YWCA gymnastics class last summer. It had been her mother's idea. "You just *think* you're uncoordinated," Mrs. Keddie had said. "I bet you'd be good at athletics if you focused on one thing and gave it a proper try."

That was one bet lost. Hannah had hated the class so much that her mother had let her drop it after the second session. There were some things, Hannah had concluded, that her body wasn't meant to do. Vaulting over a horse was one. Vaulting over a buck was another. At least last summer Hannah had failed in front of strangers. Now she would fail in front of all the girls in her class.

"Let's limber up with some somersaults," said Miss Kendall, the girls' gym teacher. She demonstrated a perfect forward somersault on the mat. One by one, everyone in the class followed suit, Caitie and Dawn first, of course. Hannah hung back till last. Then she squatted down, made herself into a miserable ball, and flopped over. She heard Dawn snicker.

"Come on, Hannah," Miss Kendall said. "Give it another try."

As the rest of the class watched, Hannah performed another sorry flop. Miss Kendall started the others on backward somersaults, while she gave Hannah some individual help. It didn't do any good.

"I can't do somersaults," Hannah said, as if offering an explanation.

"We'll try again next week," Miss Kendall said, but she sounded less perky and confident than usual. "Okay, girls, let's start on the equipment. How many of you have had gymnastics before?"

Three-quarters of the hands went up, including Dawn's and Caitie's.

"Caitie, would you demonstrate a leapfrog vault for us on the buck?"

With Miss Kendall spotting, Caitie ran up to the buck and soared high over the top, as if propelled by an invisible pogo stick. How could it look so easy when Caitie did it?

This time several girls were awkward in their first attempt, and Hannah began to feel a little better, until her turn came. Her first attempt hardly counted as an attempt at all. She ran up to the buck and stopped, unable to will herself to make the leap. It wasn't fear that stopped her as much as the hopelessness of it all. The other girls seemed to have springs in their sneakers. In hers Hannah had leaden weights.

In line for their second attempt, Dawn whispered something to Caitie. Both girls laughed. Hannah was sure they were laughing at her, and her cheeks burned.

"We'll try again next week," Miss Kendall repeated with a sigh. Couldn't she just mark an F in her grade book next to Hannah's name and be done with it?

"Klutzy Keddie," Dawn called out. "Keddie the Klutz."

"That's enough of that," Miss Kendall said, but not before a wave of giggles had passed among the girls.

The bell rang. *Thank you, bell, thank you, thank you!* Unathletic as she was, Hannah sprinted for the door before Dawn and Caitie could tease her anymore. Her only hope now was that burglars would break into Greenwood Park School some night soon, very soon, and cart all the gymnastics apparatus a thousand miles away.

5

Hannah resolutely ignored Caitie all afternoon, but when she climbed down from the school bus the next morning, a small figure in a bright pink parka hurried across the parking lot to her.

"Don't mind Dawn," Caitie said, out of breath from running. "I mean, what she said yesterday in gym. She says things, but she doesn't really mean them. Come on, we need your opinion on something."

But you laughed, too, Hannah wanted to say. Then again, she didn't know for a fact that Caitie had been laughing at *her.* Unwillingly, she let Caitie lead her across the playground to where Dawn was standing with another popular girl, Samantha Metcalf.

As Hannah approached, she had the sudden feeling that her coat was wrong. It was a heavy wool poncho her father had brought back from a trip to Mexico, not a shiny, brightly colored down ski parka like the other girls wore. Dawn rolled her eyes at Hannah's arrival, but Caitie acted as if she didn't notice.

"Okay, Hannah, here's the problem. Sam likes Roger Thornblatt, and she doesn't want him to know, but Brian stole Sam's notebook yesterday, and it had lots of stuff about Roger written in the margins. You know, like sample wedding invitations."

"I don't *know* if Brian saw them, but he *might* have, and if he did, he told *Roger,* and some of the things were—oh, I'll *die* if Brian saw them, you guys. I'll really, truly *die!*"

Hannah didn't know why it was so terrible to let a boy know you liked him, if you *did* like him. And she didn't know why anyone would get a crush on Roger Thornblatt. He was nice enough looking, she guessed, but not really handsome like Justin Seavey, or funny like Brian Taylor, or a talented musician like Michael Malone. But she knew better than to ask any questions.

"You're overreacting, Sam," Dawn said sternly, "as usual. And you practically invited Brian to steal your notebook. You know you did. You left it lying right where he'd see it, and you had CONFIDENTIAL— KEEP OUT! written all over the cover. All of this is your own fault. You have no one to blame but yourself."

"I know." Sam accepted Dawn's scolding meekly. "But what am I going to *do?*"

"I have an idea," Caitie said. "What if you pretended you did it all on purpose?"

"What do you mean?" Sam asked.

"Pretend you wrote those things, and got Brian to steal your notebook, and tell them all to Roger, so Roger will *think* you like him, but you really don't."

"Why would she do that?" Dawn asked scornfully.

Why, indeed? Hannah couldn't help but share Dawn's reaction.

"To make Michael Malone jealous!" Caitie cried in triumph. "Sam pretended she liked *Roger* just to make *Michael* jealous!"

"But isn't Michael going to think I like *him*, then?" Sam wanted to know.

"Yes, but it won't matter, because you *don't*."

"Caitie, you're a genius!" Sam said. Even Dawn looked impressed at this elegant solution to Sam's predicament.

"But how do I make Brian think I did it all on purpose?" Sam asked then.

The bell rang.

"To be continued," Caitie said in a dramatic voice. "Stay tuned for the next thrilling episode of *The Perils of Samantha Metcalf*."

Did Hannah want to stay tuned? She certainly hadn't guessed that conversations about boys could be so complicated and involved: She practically had a headache from trying to follow all the twists and turns of the backward logic of Caitie's master plan. Plus, all this elaborate scheming was only to get some silly boy to think a silly thing that wasn't even true. It was hard not to see it as a waste of Caitie's time and talent.

But would the plan work? Hannah was beginning to be interested in the answer in spite of herself.

The library was closed that day at lunch because of a special program for the lower grades. For the first time since before Christmas, Hannah walked down to the cafeteria with the rest of her class. At first she felt overwhelmed: She had forgotten the noise, the confusion, the constant reprimands from the harried cafeteria monitors. And of course she had no one to sit with. But she carried her lunch bag to a table by the window, planning to read the first few chapters of her new library book while she ate.

"Hannah! We're over here!" Caitie called to her from the popular girls' table on the other side of the room. Hannah couldn't very well refuse to join them. Slowly she made herself cross the room and take a seat next to Caitie.

It was now clear that Brian had indeed seen Sam's notebook entries about Roger. He had been reciting bits and pieces of them all morning long. "I love love *love* Roger Thornblatt!" Hannah had heard him squeal in a high-pitched voice. "Oooh, I love love love love *love* him!"

"Brian's never going to think you wrote those things on purpose if you keep blushing and carrying on when he quotes them," Dawn said once the girls were settled at their table.

"I can't help it!" Sam said. "He makes me so *mad*!"

"Unless—" Caitie paused, thinking. "Well, that could be part of the act, too, couldn't it?"

"It's some act, that's all I can say." Dawn snorted. "The envelope, please. And the Oscar for Best Actress goes to . . . Samantha Metcalf! For playing . . . herself!"

"Okay," Caitie said. "It's time for the 'act' to end. Sam has to start dropping hints that all of this is a plot to get *Michael.* So, how?"

"A familiar question," Dawn said. "Isn't this where we ended up this morning?"

"I was thinking that one of us could just *tell* Brian," Caitie went on. "You know, call Brian aside, like we have a big confidential thing to whisper in his ear. I'll do it."

"No," Dawn said. "You can't talk to boys like that. Unless the boy's your boyfriend. And none of us really have boyfriends. Yet. We have to make it that Brian finds out it was all done on purpose, but by accident. I mean, he finds out by accident that Sam did it on purpose, but his accidentally finding out is on purpose, too, only he doesn't find *that* out. Accidentally *or* on purpose. Am I making myself clear?"

The others nodded. Hannah's head whirled.

"What if—" Caitie had another brainstorm breaking. "We could pretend that we were talking about it by ourselves, but somewhere where Brian would over-hear us."

"I can't," Sam said flatly. "I'd get all confused and say the wrong thing. I know I would."

Hannah had an idea then, but she felt shy about saying it. On the other hand, she couldn't very well sit there for the whole lunch period like a big silent lump and not say *anything.*

"What if," Hannah plunged ahead, "you wrote it out ahead of time? And practiced it, like a play."

A play! The others pounced on her suggestion with delight.

"Let's work on it at my house, after school today," Caitie said. "Can you guys make it? Dawn? Sam? Hannah?"

"I can't," Dawn said. "I have a gymnastics work-out."

"I can't, either," Sam said. "I have to have the rubber bands put on my braces."

"Well, Hannah and I can get it started at least. Okay, Hannah?"

Hannah struggled to think of her own excuse: *I have homework to do? My mother is helping me make a dress for one of my dolls?* She'd have to do better than that. And maybe she *should* go. She could tell Caitie wasn't going to give her any peace until she did.

Dawn shot Caitie a look of annoyance then, as if to say, *Why are you knocking yourself out to be friends with someone like her?* The look helped Hannah to decide.

"Fine," she said. "As a matter of fact, I'm free today."

"Roll over, Shakespeare," Caitie said as they carried their trays to the conveyor belt. "Broadway, here we come!"

6

It was beginning to snow for the second time that week when Hannah and Caitie set out from Greenwood Park together. The sky was white and low, like a thick bandage of cotton gauze. The falling flakes were fine and sharp this time, icy splinters on Hannah's tongue.

Both girls walked along with their heads back and tongues poked out to catch the flakes as they fell. Then Caitie began singing the first bars of "Sleigh Ride," and Hannah joined in, her alto blending perfectly with Caitie's sweet soprano. To Hannah's surprise, Caitie knew all the words to all the verses, just as she did. When they finished one song, they sang another: "Frosty the Snowman," "Jingle Bells," "Winter Wonderland."

Half an inch of fresh snow covered the sidewalks by the time the girls arrived at Caitie's house. The Crystals lived in a large two-story house, set back from the road, with white columns in front like ones Hannah had seen at Mount Vernon. An older woman, wearing a print housedress, greeted them at the door.

"Rita!" Caitie hugged her. "This is my friend, Hannah. She's the best artist in the school."

Hannah blushed.

"Hello, Hannah," Rita said warmly. She had a lilting foreign accent. "No wet things in the house, Caitie. Off with them here. How about some hot chocolate and leftover birthday cake? I'll bring you a tray upstairs."

"My father's birthday was yesterday," Caitie explained, shedding her boots and parka. "He was forty. He took it pretty hard. He thinks forty's old. He's a cardiologist. He's a world expert on something to do with the valves of the heart. My mom's a doctor, too. She's not a world expert yet, but she's working on it. She's an ophthalmologist. That's the fancy name for eye doctor. It's not the same thing as an optometrist or optician. She gets mad if people get them mixed up and think she's an optometrist or optician instead. Only an ophthalmologist is an M.D."

Caitie certainly knew a lot about doctors. "Do you want to be a doctor, too?" Hannah asked.

"Are you kidding? Doctors are *never* home. At least my parents aren't. My father wasn't home until nine last night, and that was on his *birthday.* I'd like to be a model, except that I'm too short. And you really have to be gorgeous to be a model. But they get, like, five hundred dollars an hour. So I could work one hour a week, or two maybe, and that would be it."

"What would you do the rest of the time?"

"Everything! I'd be famous and have a lot of boy-friends and go with them to Paris or Greece or the Virgin Islands. And if I had kids I'd *see* them. I'd be there every day when they came home from school. They'd tell me all about their teachers and their friends and the boys they like, and I'd listen and help them figure out what to do. Like, if I had a daughter, and she liked Brian Taylor, I'd help her figure out what to do to get him to like her back."

"Do you like Brian Taylor?"

"No!" Caitie said emphatically. "Let's go upstairs. I'll show you my room."

Caitie's room was spacious and pretty. Everything in it matched: the bedspread and the curtains and the ruffle on the little table in front of the mirror.

"That's my vanity. *Vanity* is just the name for it. It doesn't mean you're vain or anything. That's where I sit to fix my hair and put on my makeup. And do my nails—when I'm not doing them in Mrs. McCloskey's class or Mr. Blake's office." Caitie laughed wickedly.

Hannah called her mother to say she'd be home late, and then Rita arrived with their snack. Hannah let the first sip of steaming hot chocolate slide down slowly and warm her all over.

"Do you ever wear makeup?" Caitie asked Han-nah, studying her from across the room as if for the first time. "Does your mother let you? Mine says I can wear lip gloss and a teensy-weensy bit of mascara, but that's all, at least to school. I can't wear real makeup, like eye shadow and foundation, until I'm sixteen. Except for fun, you know, at home and all."

"She never said I couldn't. But—" Hannah didn't *want* to wear makeup. "My mother doesn't wear makeup, either," she confessed. "I don't think she'd know how to put it on."

"I could show you, and then you could show her."

"We'd better get to work on Samantha's play," Hannah said.

"You'd be surprised how much better you'd look with just a little mascara and eyeliner," Caitie went on. "The trouble with being a blond is that you have blond eyebrows and blond eyelashes, and your eyes get *lost.* It makes you look washed out, and you don't *have* to."

Hannah gulped down the rest of her hot chocolate. She could see now that she had made a mistake in coming.

"Sit over here, at the vanity, and I'll fix you up. It'll just take a minute. Wait till you see how easy it is."

"I don't want to," Hannah said. "I have to be home by five, and it's past four already, and we haven't even started on the play. Besides, I'm not the makeup type. Really, I'm not."

"How do you know till you try it?" Caitie asked. "We can do the play anytime, at lunch tomorrow, or over the weekend. Come on, Hannah. If you don't like it, you can wash it off."

It was too late for escape. Hannah sat down at Caitie's vanity, trying not to think of the social studies report she could have been writing and her waiting sketch pad.

"Okay, mascara." Caitie searched the jumble of tubes and bottles in front of her. "We'll try Luscious Mink. And something in a blue for eye shadow, to bring out the blue in your eyes. For lipstick? Hmm. How about Wild Raspberry?" Caitie uncapped the lipstick, made a streak of bold color on the back of her hand, and held it out for Hannah to see. "We'll do the eyeliner first. Hold still, and keep your eyes open."

Hannah couldn't help it: As the eyeliner pencil approached her unprotected eye, she jerked her head away and squinched both eyes shut.

"*Han*-nah!"

Hannah gripped the edge of the vanity tightly and let Caitie try again. But it was like having eye surgery without any anesthetic. She couldn't make herself go through with it. No matter how she tried to hold still, at the crucial moment she would wrench her head away to save herself. To her surprise, she almost felt guilty for disappointing Caitie.

"Forget the eyeliner. For *now.*" Caitie didn't sound discouraged. "For the mascara part, you can close your eyes."

It was easier to be made up with eyes shut. Caitie

applied the mascara, and then the eye shadow, with deft, small brush strokes.

"You can open your eyes, but don't look in the mirror until we do the lipstick." Caitie outlined Hannah's mouth with a sticky smear of Wild Raspberry. "Now blot your lips together, like this. Oh, Hannah! But, wait, let's undo your braid."

Caitie shook out Hannah's long light hair, crinkly from having been braided when wet. "You could use a good haircut, if you don't mind my saying so. If you get a makeover in a magazine, the first thing they always do is cut all your hair off."

"Well, I'm not letting anybody cut mine," Hannah said. She had worn her hair in a long braid as far back as she could remember.

"Are you ready? One, two, three—ta-dah!" Caitie whirled the vanity stool around so that Hannah faced the mirror.

The old Hannah stared at the new Hannah, who stared back at her from romantic dark-lashed eyes. It was like meeting a long-lost twin, separated at birth and reared a continent apart.

"What do you think? Do you like it?"

Hannah didn't know. She would never have guessed that she could look so pretty, but she looked *old,* and somehow hard, not a little girl at all. It was as if she had been ten one minute and was sixteen the next, suddenly a teenager, old enough for a learner's driving permit, old enough to kiss a boy.

"You should definitely wear mascara," Caitie pronounced. "I don't know about the Wild Raspberry lipstick. It's a little dark for you. Let's try Wild Strawberry next time."

Next time. There wasn't going to *be* a next time, Hannah reminded herself.

"Come on, I want to show Rita. Oh, Rita!" Caitie called, pushing Hannah ahead of her down the hall. "Come see! I've made Hannah bee-you-ti-ful!"

7

After Rita and Caitie dropped her off at home, Hannah stood for a moment in the doorway, wondering what her mother was going to think about her new, grown-up look. Caitie's mother might disapprove of fifth graders wearing makeup, but Hannah thought her mother would probably laugh, the way she laughed at the articles about fashion makeovers that she skimmed while in the supermarket checkout lines. Though maybe she wouldn't laugh when she actually *saw* Hannah, looking so old, so different. And Hannah wasn't sure she *wanted* her mother to laugh.

"Hannah! I'm here, on the sun porch!" her mother called out.

"Coming!" On a sudden impulse, Hannah darted into the downstairs bath and carefully wiped off the lipstick and eye makeup. Then she headed for the porch.

Sometimes Hannah's mother was still in her studio when Hannah got home from school, but if her work for the day had gone well, she usually stopped in time to watch the four o'clock movie on TV. The Keddies' small TV was only black and white, but most of the movies Hannah's mother liked were black and white, too—old movies, and *sad* ones. Hannah's mother had devised her own rating system for movies, based on how much they made her cry. A one-hanky movie was hardly sad at all; a four-hanky movie was about as sad as a movie could be.

Hannah could tell that day's movie was a four-hanky one. Tears streamed silently down her mother's cheeks as a tough-looking man and an extremely beautiful woman sat looking into each other's eyes late at night in a deserted cafe. Hannah could imagine a boy's looking that way at Caitie someday.

"What's so sad about this movie?" she asked during the next commercial. "It looks pretty romantic to me."

"That's just it," Hannah's mother said, wiping her eyes. "It's so romantic, and their romance is doomed. *Casablanca,* with Humphrey Bogart and Ingrid Bergman. One of the all-time soggiest. Did you have fun with your friend?" Her mother kept the question casual, as if Hannah visited a different friend every day.

Despite the nonprying tone, Hannah knew her mother expected her to tell her all about it, the way she always told her all about everything. But for some reason this time she didn't feel like sharing any details.

"Uh-huh," she said.

"Do invite her here, if you'd like. Your father or I'd be happy to give her a ride home."

"Maybe," Hannah said. Her parents would have to act a lot more normal if someone like Caitie Crystal came over. Her mother couldn't cry over movies, and her father couldn't sit lost in an astronomy journal.

"Don't worry. I promise not to put on any four-hanky movies when she's here."

So her mother understood. "Oh, Mom," Hannah said. She kissed her mother's wet cheek and left her to watch the rest of Ingrid Bergman's doomed romance.

The next morning, Caitie waved to Hannah across the playground, and still to her surprise, Hannah found herself once again a member of the small group of popular girls. She was the tallest of the four, but she felt as if she were the youngest by years. Where did girls like this learn what they knew—about which pants went with which sweater, which rock group was the best, which boys were acceptable to like? There must be a big book somewhere that even Mrs. Tomacki hadn't read: *The Popular Girls' Book of Opinions about Everything.*

"I told them we didn't get a chance to write the play yesterday," Caitie told Hannah during the first break in the conversation. "So we'll do it today at lunch. Okay?"

At lunch I work in the library, Hannah was about to remind her. But Mrs. Tomacki wouldn't mind if she missed one day.

It felt odd, though, to walk right past the library at eleven-thirty without even a quick hello to her friend. Maybe Mrs. Tomacki *would* worry about why she hadn't come. But Hannah kept on going with the others, this time carrying her lunch automatically to their table.

In giggles and whispers, they worked on the play for the whole lunch period. Caitie came up with most of the lines, with help from Dawn and Samantha, and Hannah scribbled them down as fast as she could at the back of Caitie's notebook. Then, as the others listened to Sam's latest worries about Roger, Hannah neatly copied the play on another piece of paper. It amused her to set it up on the page as a real script with stage directions, just as she remembered from the plays her fourth-grade class had put on last year in Massachusetts.

When she was done, the girls pored over it, shrieking with laughter at their own wit.

"It's perfect," Caitie said. "Maybe I should be a playwright instead of a model."

During the afternoon, they slipped the play secretly from one desk to another, so each girl could make a copy. They planned to memorize their lines over the weekend, rehearse the play on Monday, and perform it on Tuesday. Even Hannah had several lines to speak.

What a strange week it had been! In one week, Hannah had been sent to the principal's office, she had worn lipstick and eye makeup, she had helped to write a play all about boys, and she had gone after school to a real live friend's house—to Caitie Crystal's house, no less. Not that Caitie was really Hannah's friend. They had nothing in common, except being new in school. Caitie cared about makeup, clothes, and boys; Hannah cared about books, art, and make-believe. And yet, oddly enough, it seemed that Caitie was becoming a friend in spite of everything. At least she was the reason that during silent reading that afternoon, Hannah sat looking out at yesterday's snow and grinning.

8

On Saturday morning, the phone rang at Hannah's house.

"It's for you, Hanniken," Hannah's father called upstairs.

For her? It was never for her. Shyly, Hannah picked up the receiver on the extension in her parents' room.

"Hi, Hannah, it's me." Caitie. "What are you doing this afternoon?"

"Nothing." Reading, painting, walking in the snow.

"Can I come over?"

"Here?" Hannah fought back panic.

"To your house."

"It's far—it's the last house on the school-bus line."

"I *know*. We drove you home on Thursday, remember? So, like after lunch? At twoish? Okay?"

"Okay," Hannah said. What else could she say? She had four hours to transform her house into a regular house, her room into a regular room, and her parents into regular parents.

But even as she figured the time, she knew it wasn't enough. Four months, four years, would hardly have been adequate. The house—she'd practically have to tear it down and build a new one. It had been built over three different centuries, and the additions made to the original pre–Revolutionary War farmhouse had created certain architectural peculiarities. To get to Hannah's room, for example, you had to walk through a bathroom; to get to her mother's studio, you had to pull down a trapdoor in the ceiling and climb a folding ladder. The floors slanted, and the walls sloped. Some rooms were painted unusual colors, a leftover eccentricity of the previous owner, who had fancied a turquoise dining room and a living room all in purple. And the furniture was a motley collection of valuable antiques mingled together with Goodwill castaways.

At least Hannah could do something about her own room; at least she could hide her dolls. But when she picked up Judith to banish her to the guest room, she was seized by the wrongness of what she had been about to do. Judith *lived* here; it was her room, too. Dolls, for Hannah, weren't *things,* to be stuffed out of sight when company came. Hannah wouldn't hurt a doll's feelings for all the Caitie Crystals and Dawn

Kleins in the world. Her room would have to stay as it was. She'd just try not to let Caitie see it, that was all.

At ten past two, the doorbell chimed, and it was Caitie.

"In your yard!" she said, bursting with excitement. "There's a great big castle, and an Easter basket with a rabbit in it, and a whole family of ducks, you know, like in *Make Way for Ducklings.*"

Hannah explained about the snow sculptures.

"You made them? Your parents, too? Did you have a kit or something?"

Hannah tried to imagine what a snow-sculpture kit would have in it. Instructions, maybe, and some enormous aluminum molds of duck and bunny and basket and castle shapes.

"We just made them up. Out of our heads."

Caitie loved the inside of the house, too. "Your living room's purple! I never saw a purple living room before. Where did you get your furniture? Nothing matches anything else, and yet it all kind of fits together."

Hannah's mother appeared, to Hannah's relief dressed presentably in a pair of jeans and an Icelandic wool sweater. Hannah hoped her mother wouldn't linger to talk to Caitie, and she didn't. She brought the girls thick wedges of fresh-baked apple pie and then obligingly left them alone again.

Caitie turned to Hannah. "But your mom's

pretty! You said she didn't know how to wear makeup, so I kind of figured—but I like how she looks. Do you think she'd let me use some mousse on her hair? It'd give it a little more body, and if she wants to try one of my lipsticks—but first I want to see your room."

"Well, it's not really . . . seeable." Hannah tried to think of a plausible excuse. "It's a mess right now."

"I don't mind mess. Is it upstairs?"

Caitie started up the stairs, with Hannah in pursuit. She poked her head into the first door on her right. "Your parents' room. Your mom's a quilt nut, isn't she? But where's your room?"

Hannah might as well get it over with.

"Through the bathroom? *That's* funny. Oh, Hannah! I like it. I really do!"

It *was* a pretty room, with windows on three sides and a cheerful braided rug on the floor. Hannah's sketches and drawings were tacked to the big corkboard that hung by her old-fashioned rolltop desk. Judith and Dorothy sat side by side on the window seat in front of the big bay window; Hannah's other dolls lined the top of the bureau or reclined on Hannah's brass bed.

"You still have your dolls! They're extra-nice ones, aren't they? I like this one best." Caitie picked up Judith. She lifted the doll's frilly petticoats to inspect the pantaloons underneath.

Hannah was affronted on Judith's behalf. Dolls

had to suffer such insults to their dignity. But at the same time she felt a rush of love for Caitie for liking her yard, her house, her mother, her room. And for noticing that Judith wasn't just any old doll, but *the* doll, the one that mattered.

"That's Judith," Hannah said. "She's the one I . . . well, that I play with most." There, she had said it.

"Play with? Like how?" Caitie sounded genuinely interested.

It was hard to explain. It wasn't that Hannah actually *played* with her dolls. She talked to them, and sat them in chairs, and, well, just *cared* about them.

"Didn't you ever have dolls?" she asked Caitie.

"Barbies. A long time ago. When I was in second grade I had twenty-three Barbies, and I had all their clothes and Barbie's Dream House and everything. But I had only one Ken. That's funny, isn't it? But it was nice for Ken, I guess. I used to put their clothes on and take them off, and I'd do things to their hair. I ruined about three Barbies that way, by chopping all their hair off or trying to dye it with melted-down crayons. I had the most Barbies of anyone in my school. The girl who had the second most, Janie Herbert, had nineteen. But then when I was in third grade, Barbies weren't cool anymore, so I stopped bringing them in."

"Where are they now?"

"Somewhere," Caitie said with an airy vagueness that horrified Hannah. "I think Rita put them in a box in the back of my closet."

In a *box.* It always broke Hannah's heart to hear about mistreated or abandoned dolls.

"So do you dress yours up and stuff?" Caitie asked.

"Sort of. Sometimes I put on their best clothes, and we have tea parties, with tiny pink-frosted cakes."

"Let's have one now!" Caitie looked ready to fly downstairs for the tea things. "Are the cakes real or pretend?"

"Real, but—" It would be too strange to have a doll tea party with Caitie Crystal. "We don't have anything ready. Maybe some other time."

"How about tomorrow? Can I bring my Barbies? I think I still have clothes for most of them."

"Of course," Hannah said.

"Some of them aren't really Barbies," Caitie confessed, as if that might lead Hannah to change the invitation. "Some are Skippers. You know, she's Barbie's little sister."

"That's all right," Hannah said grandly. "Bring them all."

"All? Even Ken?"

Hannah knew too well what it was like to be the excluded one. "Even Ken," she said.

9

Hannah's mother helped her bake the tea cakes: sugar cookies, rolled thin and cut out with a thimble. Together they spread a dab of pink icing on each one and transferred them carefully to a small doily-covered plate.

"Somehow I wouldn't have thought Caitie was the tea-party type," her mother said, handing Hannah the icing spoon to lick.

Until yesterday, Hannah hadn't thought Caitie was the tea-party type, either, but now she found herself annoyed at her mother's comment. Was Caitie supposed to be too grown-up to be the tea-party type? What did that make Hannah? And what was the tea-party *type,* anyway?

"Well, it was Caitie's idea," she said stiffly, and stuck the spoon in the sink with the icing still on it.

An hour before the tea party, Hannah dressed her large doll family in their fanciest clothes. Some of the dolls were so old and battered that party clothes only made them look more brave and forlorn.

Judith was one of the few dolls who had come to Hannah brand new, a Christmas present from her parents four years ago. Judith had been, and was still, the most beautiful doll Hannah had ever seen. She stood two feet high, and her arms and legs were jointed in all the right places so she could sit on a chair or sip from a teacup. Her hair was soft and curly, a rich deep brown, and the expression on her face was sweet and intelligent. It was impossible to talk to Judith and not believe that she was listening and understanding and thinking her own secret thoughts about what you had said. However old Hannah was, Judith seemed just the same age. When Hannah had been seven, Judith had seemed seven, too. Now Judith seemed ten and a half.

Hannah and Judith had matching blue velvet party dresses with white lace collars. Once they were both dressed, each with a blue velvet bow in her hair, Hannah felt ready for the party, ready to serve as hostess to twenty-three Barbies and one Ken.

When Caitie arrived, just past two o'clock, she was carrying a large cardboard carton. But she must have caught on to how Hannah felt about dolls, because the Barbies were standing up in the box, shoulder to shoulder, not lying in a jumbled heap.

"I *missed* my Barbies!" Caitie said as she began unpacking them in Hannah's room. "See, I brushed their hair and everything."

Long, lustrous curls streamed down over the Barbies' shoulders, but the dolls wore the oddest assortment of clothes Hannah had ever seen in a group of party guests: everything from a frilly pink prom dress to a bright orange bikini to an astronaut suit. Three Barbies had no clothes at all, but were wrapped in scraps of fabric, secured with safety pins.

"And he-e-e-re's Ken!" Caitie crowed, lifting the last doll from the box. "I made him wear his tuxedo."

Caitie herself had on skinny black pants and an oversized neon green sweater. Dawn and Samantha had lots of outfits just like it. "I should have worn a dress," Caitie said apologetically, looking over at Hannah and Judith.

It was the first time in Hannah's life that someone had taken *her* as the standard for how to dress.

"You look fine. Really," she told Caitie. "This way the Barbies who don't have on dresses won't feel bad."

Caitie laughed. "We can pretend it's a costume party. Or a come-as-you-are party! You know, where you have to wear exactly what you were wearing when you got the invitation. Except that if you were in the shower, you don't have to come naked. You can wear a towel. So, like, the astronaut Barbie was in the middle of a trip to the moon when she got her invitation, and the bikini Barbie was sunbathing on her deck."

"What about these?" Hannah pointed to the three fabric-draped Barbies.

"Maybe they were taking showers, only instead of towels they grabbed pieces of fabric."

"Or they could be models working for a fabric designer," Hannah suggested.

"Or, like they have nudist colonies? Where people don't wear any clothes? Well, maybe these Barbies live in a *fabric* colony, where instead of clothes everybody wears pieces of fabric."

This set off the girls laughing uncontrollably, the way they had the first day outside Mr. Blake's office. When one would begin to recover, the other would launch into a new spasm of laughter, setting off the first one again. Then, as suddenly as they had begun, they were done.

"It wasn't that funny," Caitie said, puzzled.

"I know," Hannah said, wiping her eyes.

Hannah didn't have chairs for everyone, so most of the Barbies sat on the rug, their legs sticking out stiff and straight in front of them. (Ken preferred to stand.) Hannah and Caitie poured tea from the porcelain doll teapot into tiny teacups and helped the Barbies pretend to sip. Since the dolls couldn't really eat their pink-frosted cakes, the girls ate the cakes for them.

When every crumb was gone, and all the tea as well, Caitie wandered over to look at the sketches tacked to Hannah's corkboard.

"Where's my picture?" she wanted to know. "I

forgot all about it. The picture of me—you never finished it."

"It's almost finished," Hannah said. She had worked some more on it, but then had stopped, afraid of spoiling what she had already done.

"Where is it?"

"On my drawing table. Wait, I'll get it."

Caitie was already perched on Hannah's stool, peering intently at the drawing on the top of Hannah's pile, the one of Hildegarde the cat looking out at the snow.

Hannah tugged at the legs of her white tights, which had begun to sag around the ankles. It made her feel suddenly shy to have Caitie looking at her pictures, even the unfinished ones and the false starts, the ones that weren't any good.

"This is like the cover of a magazine," Caitie said, holding the cat drawing at arm's length to see it better. "My parents get this magazine called *The New Yorker.* It comes every week, and there's always a picture on the cover, just like this."

"A picture of a cat looking out at the snow?" Hannah knew that wasn't what Caitie meant, but Caitie's praise embarrassed her.

"No, not a cat, but—you'd have to see them. They're pretty. They make you happy when you look at them. Just like this one." Forgetting that she was supposed to be looking for the other sketch, Caitie slid off the stool, still clutching the Hildegarde drawing.

"I have an idea," she announced. "Let's send your picture to *The New Yorker* for them to make into a cover."

"I don't want to," Hannah said, but she could tell Caitie wasn't listening.

"I'll do it. I'll get the address out of one of the magazines at home. I should write the letter to go with it, too, in case they think it's conceited for you to send in your own picture. You know, like you can't nominate yourself for class president, so your best friend does it for you, and then you nominate her for secretary-treasurer."

"But—"

"Actually, we could get the address right now by calling the public library. Did you know that? They have this number you can call and ask them anything and they'll tell you. Except for homework. They always know when it's homework, and then they tell you to come into the library and look it up in the card catalog. The branch by my house is open Sunday afternoons till six. Where's your phone? You don't have one in your room? Is there one in your parents' room?"

Hannah managed to nod.

"You'll have to give me, like, ten percent of the money you get from *The New Yorker.* Okay? Because I'm your agent, and that's what agents get. My father wrote a book on how not to have a heart attack, and he had an agent, so I know."

Hannah gave up. She might as well let Caitie go

ahead and write her letter. But Caitie couldn't make her send her picture anywhere she didn't want it to go, any more than Mrs. Tomacki could make her enter the superintendent of schools' art contest.

Ten minutes later, Caitie had *The New Yorker*'s address, a large brown envelope and a stamp from Hannah's desk drawer, and her letter, printed neatly on a piece of notebook paper:

2734 Parkside Lane
Greenwood Park, Maryland 20950

The New Yorker
25 West 43rd Street
New York, N.Y. 10036

Dear New Yorker:

I am sending you a picture by my friend Hannah Keddie to make into a cover for your magazine. You can send the money to me because I'm her agent.

Oh, I forgot to tell you. My name is Caitie Crystal. Caitie is my nickname. My real name is Caitlin. I am ten years old.

Bye for now.

Sincerely,
Your friend,
Caitie Crystal

P.S. Write back soon!

Caitie licked the flap of the envelope and pressed it sealed with the palm of her hand. "I'll mail it on my way home. Today's Sunday, so they won't pick it up until tomorrow, and that means it'll get to New York on Wednesday, right? So if they write back right away, like I told them to, we'll get the check on Friday. Or maybe they'll call? I think they call if it's good news. So that would make it Wednesday. Three more days, then—fame and fortune!"

Hannah knew there would be no fame and fortune for her on the cover of *The New Yorker*. If a children's magazine hadn't even put her tree on its stupid kids' page, how could Caitie think a magazine for grown-ups was going to put Hildegarde the cat on the cover? It made Hannah almost sick to think of the big brown envelope lying in the bottom of a mailbox, stuffed into a big canvas sack, speeding northward in a U.S. Postal Service truck, then opened with the rest of the morning's mail in an office somewhere in New York City.

Caitie's wild dream had gone far enough. "It's my picture, Caitie," Hannah said as firmly as she could, "and I don't want to send it anywhere. I really don't."

"You have to!" Caitie waved the envelope at her. "I've already written the letter! I've already sealed the envelope!"

"Well, unseal it, then."

"I bet they'll pay you a thousand dollars for it. Nine hundred for you, and a hundred for me. I'm spending mine on boots. I already know the pair I want. I saw them last weekend at Georgetown Leather, in White Flint Mall.''

"They're not going to want it. They're *not.*" Maybe if Hannah repeated the cold truth often enough, it would eventually sink in to Caitie.

"Not if you don't send it, they're not. Believe me, my parents get that magazine. Your picture is just as good as the ones on those covers. Better, even.''

It was harder saying no to Caitie than to Mrs. Tomacki. And, well, Caitie sounded so *sure.* Her parents were famous doctors, and her father had written a book, and Caitie always knew the right clothes to wear. . . . It was ridiculous even to hope. But maybe there was some small, very small chance *The New Yorker* really would want Hannah's drawing.

No. Hildegarde the cat was not going to be on the cover of *The New Yorker* magazine. Caitie could go ahead and mail off the envelope if that's what it took to convince her, but Hannah knew better.

10

On the following Tuesday, the girls gave their performance of Samantha's play. The (imaginary) curtain rose at lunchtime, and the girls followed the script just as they had rehearsed it before school the day before.

THE PERILS OF SAMANTHA METCALF

ACT I

The curtain rises on a typical cafeteria scene. At one table Roger Thornblatt, Brian Taylor, Justin Seavey, and Michael Malone are eating their lunches. They are laughing and shoving each other and sticking french fries up their noses. At the next table Samantha Metcalf, Dawn Klein, Caitie Crystal, and Hannah Keddie are eating their lunches. They speak loudly enough to be overheard by the boys.

DAWN: It worked, Sam. Your *secret plan* was a success! [*At the words* secret plan *the boys drop their french fries and begin to listen.*]

SAM [*Laughing modestly*]: Oh, it was nothing!

CAITIE: Just the most brilliant plan ever, that's all.

DAWN: How did you ever think of writing all that lovey-dovey stuff about Roger in your notebook—

HANNAH: And leaving it for Brian to see—

CAITIE: Knowing he would tell the other boys—

HANNAH: Just to make Michael jealous!

DAWN: They fell for it, too. They really think you like Roger! [*The girls shriek with laughter at the very idea.*]

CAITIE: Boys are so dumb. Especially Brian.

DAWN: They really don't know that Sam did it all on purpose. It isn't Roger she likes at all, but Michael.

SAM [*Lovesick*]: I don't *like* Michael, I *love* him.

HANNAH: Hush! They'll hear you.

CAITIE: It doesn't matter if they do. They're so dumb.

DAWN: That's the understatement of the year.

DAWN, SAM, CAITIE, and HANNAH [*All together*]:
Boys are dumb!

The curtain falls.

The trouble was that, even though the play was done, the curtain *didn't* fall. Now what? What were the girls supposed to say next? It seemed somehow that the boys should applaud and the girls should join hands and curtsey, but of course that wasn't right.

Instead the boys just sat there, struck dumb with amazement. Roger looked undeniably relieved, while Michael looked a bit ill. The girls just sat there, too, with no script memorized for Act II.

A moment of silence, and then, mercifully, the bell rang.

"*Girls* are dumb!" Brian called out over the commotion. But it wasn't a very snappy comeback, and it had come too late.

More plays! After lunch Mrs. Harding told the class that their major language arts project for that marking period would be to write and perform skits based on the lives of famous people born in February.

"Thursday is February first," she said. "February is the birth month of two of our greatest presidents, Washington and Lincoln, but many other famous people were born in February, as well—President Ronald Reagan, the poet Langston Hughes, Susan B. Anthony, and Copernicus, to name a few. I want you to work in groups of four, two boys and two girls. You'll perform the skits in class at the end of the month."

Dawn's hand went up. "Can we pick our own groups?"

Mrs. Harding nodded. "I'll need to know who's in each group by Friday. That's all, I think. Show me how imaginative and creative you can be!"

Hannah made a series of cat doodles on the brown cover of her language arts textbook. They all looked like the Hildegarde drawing Caitie had sent to *The New Yorker.* She hated group projects. She was always chosen last for groups. Half the time she wasn't chosen at all, just bunched together at the end with the handful of other kids nobody had wanted. Then she wound up doing all the work herself, anyway, since she was usually the one who had the best ideas and cared the most about the assignment.

But this time a plump triangle of a folded note landed on her desk. When she opened it, the note said: "Be in my group, okay?" The handwriting was Caitie's.

Mrs. Harding turned to the chalkboard, and Hannah heard Brian whisper across the aisle to Caitie: "If we have to have dumb girls in our group, Michael and I figure one of them might as well be you. What do you say?"

"Well, if we have to have dumb boys in our group—well, okay."

"We? Who else is in your group?"

"Hannah."

Would Brian withdraw the invitation?

"That's okay. I think Michael would have been worried if it had been"—he lowered his voice—"you know, Sam."

Poor Sam. But maybe she could be in a group with Roger. And maybe they could do their skit on something romantic, like George Washington proposing to Martha, and maybe then—Hannah stopped, mid-thought. She never would have guessed that she could get carried away with such silliness. But she had to admit that it would be fun being in Caitie's group, working on a skit with two popular boys.

She was waiting in the bus line an hour later, studying Mrs. Harding's list of February birthdays, when she heard Dawn and Caitie walk by.

"Brian and Michael want to be in our group?" she heard Dawn squeal.

Caitie hesitated, then said something in a voice Hannah couldn't hear. But, shrinking behind two tall girls, she heard all too well what Dawn said next.

"*Hannah?* You're kidding! She's—she's a baby, Caitie. She's, like, stuck in second grade or something. You can't be serious."

"She's my friend," Caitie said staunchly. "I didn't think you'd mind. You're so popular, you can be in any group. You know you can."

"Not a group with Brian and Michael in it. Sam has her group already, too. There's nobody left except *weirdos.*" Dawn was crying now. "I was counting on you, Caitie! I mean, don't you like me anymore? Are we best friends or not?"

Then they were out of earshot. Hannah climbed aboard the bus, her heart pounding underneath her bright Mexican poncho. Dawn's cruel words repeated themselves over and over again in her echoing brain: *She's a baby, Caitie. She's, like, stuck in second grade or something.*

But that wasn't even the worst part. The worst part had been hearing the raw pain in Dawn's voice: *Don't you like me anymore?* Hannah had been so happy to be included in Caitie's group. It had never occurred to her that Dawn might then be left out.

11

It was hard agreeing on a famous February person for the group skit. Michael, who played first violin in the school orchestra, wanted the composer Felix Mendelssohn. Caitie and Brian both groaned.

"I had him in a piano lesson once," Caitie said, as if that alone were enough to condemn him.

Hannah wanted Winslow Homer, the only artist Mrs. Harding had included on the list.

"The ancient Greek guy?" Brian asked when she suggested it. "I'm not wearing a toga. No way!"

Before Hannah could explain that this was a different Homer, with no togas required, Caitie was ready with her suggestion: "George Washington."

"Bor-ing!" Michael said, and Hannah couldn't help but agree.

"But it'd be so easy," Caitie protested. "We wouldn't have to read any books or anything. We could write it right out of our heads. Cutting down the cherry tree: 'I cannot tell a lie, I did it with my little hatchet.' Then proposing to Martha. I'll be Martha, and Hannah can be—did Washington have a daughter? Or a sister? Wait: Betsy Ross! Hannah can be Betsy Ross! Okay, so then we'd have the Revolutionary War. Valley Forge. Inauguration Day. His false teeth hurt. Then he catches cold and dies. The end!"

Brian bopped Caitie over the head with the rolled-up February birthday list. "We're not doing a composer or anybody Greek, and we're not doing boring George, either. We're doing Babe Ruth, born February sixth, 1895. I'll be Babe, and Michael can pitch balls to me."

"Was Babe Ruth married?" Caitie wanted to know. "There have to be girls' parts in this, you know."

"Married? I hope not," Brian said in horror. "But we'll find something for you and Hannah. How about, you can be fans, really big fans who practically worship me. We can have a scene where you come up and beg me to autograph a baseball."

"She can be Mrs. Babe Ruth, if she wants," Michael said quickly. "And Hannah can be—"

"I'll be the narrator," Hannah said. "I'll tell what happens in between scenes."

So that was settled. Hannah glanced around the room to see how the other groups were faring. Sam had chosen Molly Davis to be her partner, and together they had managed to get Roger and handsome Justin Seavey in their group. Now that Roger knew—or thought he knew—that Sam didn't really like him, he had apparently let down his guard. Sam's group was looking at the books on Abraham Lincoln. Hannah predicted that Roger would be Abe, and Sam would be Mary Todd.

Dawn was in a group with Lizzie Haynes, Evan Dixon, and Daniel Collea. They weren't weird kids; at least Hannah didn't think so. She had sat with Lizzie on a school trip in the fall, and she remembered that Lizzie collected seashells. But of course knowing about seashells didn't count for as much as knowing about clothes and boys—though Hannah still didn't understand why.

Wednesday was P.E. day, which meant that every Wednesday for the next few weeks Hannah would have to suffer the humiliation of gymnastics. The second gymnastics class was as bad as the first. Once again, Miss Kendall started out with forward and backward somersaults. Once again, Hannah couldn't do even a simple forward roll. She managed to hoist herself up stiffly on the parallel bars, though the muscles in her arms ached and burned. She made herself inch her way across the balance beam, which looked so wide when Miss Kendall laid it on the floor and so narrow when it was raised three feet in the air. But she couldn't face the horse or the buck. Every time she ran up for her vault, she stopped before making her try.

"What's the matter?" Caitie asked her, dropping back in line at one point to stand next to Hannah. "You're not even trying."

"I am, too. I just . . . can't do it, that's all."

"Not if you just *stand* there, you can't. You have to *jump*. You have to run up and *jump*. That's all there is to it."

All there was for Caitie, maybe.

"Caitie!" Dawn called then. "Come spot me on the horse."

"Do you want me to help you?" Caitie asked Hannah. "I could stand right next to the buck and kind of, you know, give you a boost or something."

"Caitie!" Dawn called again. "We'll miss our turn."

Hannah let Caitie go. It wouldn't do any good to have Caitie help her. She could no more vault over the buck than she could fly out the window into the raw February wind.

After school that day, Dawn, Sam, and Hannah went over to Caitie's house. Hannah felt awkward having Dawn there, but she had accepted Caitie's invitation before she knew Dawn was coming.

In the Crystals' downstairs rec room, Caitie poured diet Cokes and opened a big bag of pretzels. She turned on the TV to the rock video station, and the girls sprawled on the floor in front of it. Still watching

TV, Caitie rolled up to a graceful headstand. Dawn and Samantha joined Caitie in headstands of their own. Three pairs of slim legs in skinny pants pointed toward the ceiling light fixture.

What am I supposed to do now? Hannah wondered. If she couldn't even do a somersault, she wasn't about to attempt a headstand. But it felt odd, almost impolite, to be the only one right side up.

"Did you see Mrs. McCloskey's dress yesterday?" Dawn asked, still upside down.

"The one with the big underarm stains?" Sam asked.

"Somebody should *tell* her," Dawn said.

"I like Mrs. Harding's haircut," Caitie said. "It makes her face look less round, don't you think?"

"Mr. Kovack had chalk dust on his pants again this week." Dawn was beginning to look red in the face, and her legs wobbled.

"Front or back?" Sam asked.

"Front!" Laughing now, Dawn toppled over. Sam flopped down, too. Only Caitie was left, like a mirror-image ballerina pirouetting in midair.

Hannah crunched down on the last broken pretzel from the bag. She hadn't noticed Mrs. McCloskey's underarm stains *or* Mrs. Harding's haircut *or* the chalk dust on the music teacher's pants.

"What do you think Hannah should do with *her* hair?" Caitie asked then. "All in favor of cutting it, answer aye."

Caught off guard, Hannah involuntarily clutched her braid.

"Aye," Caitie answered her own question promptly. "She'd look a lot older."

"Aye, I guess," Sam said. "But I think boys like long hair."

Dawn shrugged, as if nothing to do with Hannah was worth her attention.

"Boys *think* they like long hair," Caitie said. "But deep down they'd have to admit that most girls look better once they cut it off."

"Anyway, boys don't like braids," Sam said. "Braids are something out of *Anne of Green Gables.*"

Hannah's favorite book.

"You know who's good?" Caitie said, finally lowering herself out of her headstand. "Tiffany at the Hair Place. She's cut mine the last couple of times. I think she's better than Nicki."

"At the Cuttery they have guys cutting girls' hair and girls cutting guys' hair," Dawn said.

Sam made a face. "I wouldn't like that. I'd want a guy to see my hair *after* it was all cut and blow-dried, not *during.* I don't even want to go to a place that cuts guys' hair, too. What if I was there with my hair all wet and stringy, and Roger came in to get his hair cut and saw me like that?"

With Sam on the subject of Roger, Hannah's braid was safe. But she held on tightly to the end of it, anyway, just in case.

12

Hannah had always had mixed feelings about Valentine's Day. She loved making valentines out of construction paper and doilies and bits of satin ribbon and lace. But most kids just gave silly store-bought cards. And it was sad when the valentines were handed out at school and some kids got fewer than others. Hannah never got very many herself; most of hers came from girls whose parents made them give a valentine to everyone in the class.

This year Hannah made valentines for all the girls, including Dawn, and one for Mrs. Harding, but she made a special, extra fancy one for Caitie. She carefully cut out hearts and flowers and cupids from a sheet of shiny silver paper and mounted them on a large lace-edged red card. Caitie's valentine was beautiful enough to be on the cover of a magazine.

Hannah and Caitie hadn't heard from *The New*

Yorker yet. Over two weeks had gone by now with no phone call or letter. *Maybe they send a telegram?* Hannah had caught herself wondering. But no telegram had come, either.

On Valentine's Day morning, Hannah slipped all her cards into the large decorated mailbox in the front of Mrs. Harding's room. Just before the party, Mrs. Harding asked Justin to serve as mailman. Up and down the aisles he went, laying pink and white and red envelopes on every desk.

Hannah got eight valentines, including ones from Caitie and Sam. None from Dawn, of course, but she certainly hadn't expected one. On the bottom valentine in her pile the signature on the back had been crossed out so completely with green ballpoint pen that she couldn't tell whom it was from.

"It's from a boy," Caitie said, when Hannah showed it to her during the classroom party. "Obviously from a boy who didn't want you to know who he was. Well, first he did, and then he didn't. Your secret admirer," she said in thrilling tones.

Who could it be? Hannah wasn't sure she wanted to know. A secret admirer was practically like a doomed romance, mysterious and exciting.

"Look at the envelope," Caitie said. "He printed your name so you wouldn't be able to recognize his writing, but he used the same green ballpoint. That could be a clue. How many boys in this class use a green pen? It can't be that many. Wait. I saw someone using a green ballpoint pen just the other day. Where was it?"

"On our Babe Ruth play," Hannah said numbly.

"Michael Malone's notes! Do you have them with you?"

Hannah found them in her desk: Michael's notes from the Babe Ruth biography they had been reading together in the library.

"Does the ink match?" Caitie asked. Hannah laid the crossed-out valentine side by side with Michael's scribbled-over notes. The same pen had clearly been used for both.

A valentine from Michael Malone! Hannah hardly knew Michael, but already she liked him the best of the boys in their class. Michael went along with Brian's clowning, but Hannah could see he had a more serious side to him. He had to be serious to have learned to play the violin so well. A musician and an artist . . . But now she was being as silly as the other fifth-grade girls.

"Did you get a valentine from Brian?" Hannah asked Caitie then.

"Yes. Isn't it awful?" Caitie handed the card to Hannah. It showed a picture of an ice-cream sundae, and the printed words said, "I'm sweet on you." But Brian had inserted a handwritten NOT, so that the card read, "I'm NOT sweet on you." He had signed it, "NOT love, Your NOT-secret NOT-admirer."

"I think he likes me," Caitie said. "It's my favorite valentine, tied with yours. I'm going to save yours forever. Nobody in my other school could make valentines like that."

Dawn came over then. "I got fifteen valentines," she said smugly. "Five from boys. How many did you get, Hannah?"

Hannah refused to let Dawn make her feel bad. "I got enough," she said. She changed the subject before Caitie could tell Dawn about her valentine from Michael. "Where's Sam?"

The girls looked around the room. Sam was nowhere to be seen. "I bet she didn't get a valentine from Roger," Dawn said knowingly. "One of us'd better go to the girls' room and see if she's there crying."

"Let's all go," Caitie said. But when the girls asked Mrs. Harding for lavatory permissions, she said they'd have to go two at a time. "First you, Hannah, and Caitie."

Sure enough, they heard Samantha sobbing as soon as they'd pushed open the girls' room door.

"I didn't get a valentine from Roger, or Michael, either. Not from a single boy. And I thought Roger was starting to like me, being in the play group together. If he's going to be Abe Lincoln, with me as Mary Todd, doesn't that mean he likes me a little bit? I sent him one, and now I feel terrible. I didn't sign my name, but I know he knows it's from me. I hate him! I really do. I hate him!"

Caitie handed Sam a paper towel, soaked in cold water and wrung out to a compress. "Here. Your eyes are all red and puffy."

Sam held the towel to her eyes, then to her forehead. "Does Roger know I'm here?"

"I don't think so," Hannah said. That much was true.

"Oh, you guys, what am I going to *do*?"

"True love never runs smooth," Caitie said. "That's a quote from somewhere. You'll get over it. My cousin Bonnie went steady with six different boys when she was in the seventh grade, and she says none of them means anything to her now."

"But I haven't even gone steady *once*," Sam wailed.

"Boys grow up later than girls. That's what Bonnie says. They're, like, two years behind us. Give Roger time."

Boys are the lucky ones, Hannah thought as they walked back to Mrs. Harding's room, leading a red-nosed Samantha between them. Two years behind sounded just about right.

13

As the end of February drew near, Hannah began to worry about whether Mrs. Harding would like their Babe Ruth skit. There was too much baseball in it, and too much silliness. Brian insisted on long, drawn-out sequences in which he slammed imaginary home runs to Michael's imaginary fastballs, as if every one of Babe Ruth's 714 lifetime homers had to be acted out, one by one. Caitie insisted on an equally long scene of her own, in which Mrs. Ruth cooked huge platters of food to feed her husband's legendary appetite. Caitie was a gifted comedienne, and it *was* funny to watch her frantic pantomime of a cook gone berserk. But the cooking scene didn't really shed much light on the central accomplishments of the Sultan of Swat. With some help from Michael, Hannah wrote the overall narration, and at least that was serious and accurate. But the group would be graded as a whole.

During rehearsals Hannah stole looks at Michael Malone. Was he really her secret admirer? Every once in a while she thought she caught him looking at her, and sometimes the two of them sat quietly together, side by side, watching as Brian pretended to bonk Caitie in the head with imaginary baseballs or showed off for her how many push-ups he could do. *It's a shame,* Hannah thought, *that a boy and a girl can't just be friends, without making a big romance out of it.* In some ways she had more in common with Michael than she had with Caitie, but she couldn't imagine writing his name on every page of her notebook with hearts and flowers around it.

On the afternoon that the skits were finally performed, Hannah's group went first. The other kids laughed long and hard at Brian's baseball antics and Caitie's slapstick cooking routine. If Mrs. Harding was grading on audience appeal, they had nothing to worry about. The skits on Thomas Edison and Charles Darwin, and the ones on Reagan and Lindbergh, weren't as funny, but they were solid and well done. The Abe Lincoln skit, in Hannah's opinion, was the worst— embarrassingly bad. She could hardly bear to watch the way Samantha simpered and batted her eyelashes at poor Roger in his fake beard and stovepipe hat. The best skit turned out to be by Dawn's group, on Susan B. Anthony, with Lizzie Haynes playing the lead role. But Dawn sat down afterward without a trace of satisfaction in her expression. For her there could be no satisfaction in a skit without popular boys.

Mrs. Harding handed out the grades the next day, giving each member of the group a copy of her comments. "Babe Ruth skit; B minus," Hannah read. "Excellent narration. But, overall, humor at the expense of information."

Hannah folded the grade slip in half, and in half again, and put it away. She never got B's, except in gym, where she felt lucky to pass at all. The skit was to be half of the marking period grade for language arts. Maybe she'd get a B now on her report card. She couldn't help but feel annoyed at Caitie. They could have enjoyed doing a good job on the skit just as much as doing a poor one. She'd have to work harder now for the rest of the marking period.

"We got a B!" Caitie said as the class lined up to go to lunch.

"I know," Hannah said soberly. "I'm going to the library during lunch today. We'll have to do really well on all the other assignments if we want to bring our language arts grades back up."

"What are you talking about?" Caitie turned around, astonished. "B is great! It's terrific! My parents are getting back from a conference tonight, and they'll die for happiness when I tell them. They'll fold their hands and close their eyes and die with absolute pure joy."

"For a B?"

"Right now they'd be grateful for a C. In math,

they'd probably take a D. Even a D minus minus minus." Caitie giggled.

"But you're smart," Hannah said. She had known Caitie wasn't much of a student, but she had never imagined that her grades were so poor. "You can do better than that."

"That's what the teachers keep telling my parents. That's what drives them crazy. I'm an underachiever. I'm not realizing my academic potential." Caitie sounded almost proud as she quoted what was apparently a familiar verdict.

"Is it because you had to change schools in the middle of the year?"

"Didn't you know? Why do you think I *changed* schools? I underachieved myself right out of the Waverly School, so my parents decided to try public school instead."

Hannah was finding it hard to believe. "So you like . . . well, failed?"

"That's another word for it," Caitie said. "But now I have my big bee-you-ti-ful B. Maybe we can be in a group in math next, and I can get a couple of B's there, too."

Hannah had no intention of being in more groups that got B's. She turned down the hall toward the library.

"Where are you going?" Caitie asked.

"I told you. I'm going to the library to study."

"During *lunch*?"

"Do you want to come with me? We can get a head start on studying for the math test, too."

Caitie shook her head. "I'm not studying during *lunch*," she said crossly.

Hannah shrugged. "See you later."

"Dawn!" she heard Caitie call then. "Wait up!"

Hannah tried not to care as she saw Caitie catch up with Dawn. The sound of their laughter drifted down the hall after her. What were they laughing at together? Was it that comical for someone to want to do well in school?

In the library, Mrs. Tomacki greeted her warmly. "Welcome back, Hannah! I've missed you these past weeks. What have you been reading?"

"*The Secret Garden.* It's wonderful! Especially the part where—but I can't really talk today. Can I eat my lunch here while I study?"

Mrs. Tomacki nodded. "Now, you haven't forgotten about the superintendent of schools' art contest, have you? Your work has to be submitted in another month or so."

"I'm not—I mean, I'm still thinking about it."

Not that she was going to change her mind. It was bad enough that she had let Caitie talk her into sending the Hildegarde picture off to *The New Yorker.* But if the people at the magazine didn't want it—and it was plain now that they didn't—why didn't they at least mail it back? Unless . . . No, it couldn't be that they did want it. Still, it had been a whole month, and a month was so long.

Hannah felt like telling Mrs. Tomacki about it, but she was too embarrassed. Besides, Hannah had come to the library to study. She *had* to study now, or else she'd get her first B ever in language arts.

Thanks a lot, Caitie, Hannah said to herself, opening *Adventures in Language Arts* to the chapter on periods and commas. *Thanks a lot.*

14

Spring came earlier in Maryland, Hannah noticed, than it had in Massachusetts. By the first of March the snow had melted, and the forsythia were beginning to bud and bloom. But the stars were the same in both places, following one another across the sky season by season, exactly on schedule. On cold winter nights the sky was dominated by Orion, with his bright starry belt. But by early March he appeared lower and lower in the sky, and when Hannah and her father went out for a late night walk they began to look instead for Leo the Lion and Virgo.

"How did your group make out with the skit?" Hannah's father asked her when they were out walking next. "I don't think you ever told us what Mrs. Harding thought of it."

"We got a B. Well, actually a B minus. But she said the narration—that was my part—was excellent."

Hannah's father gave a gentle tug on her braid to slow her down. "There's Mars, just below Regulus." Hannah peered through her binoculars. The red color of the planet was easy to see, especially on a moonless night.

"Were you disappointed in your grade?" her father asked. "It sounds to me like the other kids kind of let you down."

"A little bit." Not disappointed, really—given how the rehearsals had gone, she had hardly expected any better—but annoyed and irritated at Caitie. Yet now Hannah found herself wanting to defend Caitie against her father's implied criticism. "It wasn't like that. We—they were just having fun. Caitie isn't really *into* school, if you know what I mean."

"What is she *into*?"

"Oh, clothes, I guess, and boys."

Even as she said it, Hannah realized that the answer made Caitie sound like a shallow, silly person. And she wasn't. Not really. Samantha was silly, and Dawn, too, worse than silly—Dawn was selfish, even cruel. But Caitie—it was hard to make her father understand that Caitie was different from the others, funnier and more free spirited. Caitie was smart, even if she was lazy. She cared about people.

Hannah's father stopped to watch two squirrels chase each other up an oak tree. "I don't know, Hanniken," he said. "She somehow doesn't sound like your kind of kid. Of course, nowadays half the kids don't sound like *kids* at all. Just be careful, all right? Popularity isn't everything. You don't want to let your schoolwork suffer. Or lose sight of who *you* are."

"I won't," Hannah said, impatient with her father's lecturing tone. She scuffed at a tuft of muddy grass with the toe of her duck boot. "I won't. I promise."

Usually another sign of spring was that the girls' gym classes at Hannah's various schools started heading outside for softball. Hannah loved being outdoors, and she hated softball least of all the year's gym activities. The softball teams tended to be large, and Hannah would volunteer to stand farthest out in the outfield, with last ups. With any luck, no balls got hit her way and the period would end before her turn at bat ever came. For Hannah a softball game meant standing alone in a field of dandelions, sketching pictures in her head.

This year there was still one last gymnastics class to be survived. Hannah had learned that the only way to get through those humiliating forty-five minutes every week was to pretend that the whole thing was a movie she was watching, a movie with some clumsy stranger in it, who despite certain physical similarities had nothing to do with *her,* the real Hannah.

After six weeks of Miss Kendall's patient coaching, Hannah's forward somersaults had improved a little bit, and she was no worse than a few of the other girls on the parallel bars and the balance beam. But the buck and the horse still defeated her utterly. It was as if there were an invisible live wire placed in front of them, stopping her with an electric jolt every time she ran up for her turn at a vault.

This last week of gymnastics was no exception.

Jump! Hannah willed herself to make one final attempt. But she didn't jump. She stopped in her tracks at the same invisible line. There. It was over at least, over for another year.

The bell rang, dismissing the class for lunch, dismissing the class, as far as Hannah was concerned, forever. But as she turned to line up with the others, she felt Caitie's hand on her arm.

"Wait a minute," Caitie said. "Miss Kendall? Can we stay and try the buck just one more time? Hannah and me?"

"It's not going to do any good," Hannah said. Besides, gymnastics was *over.*

But Miss Kendall laid down her clipboard and grinned at Caitie. "I can't let you use the equipment alone, but I can stay with you for a little while. Maybe between the two of us, Caitie, we can get Hannah over this thing."

She and Caitie stationed themselves on either side of the buck. "Come on, Hannah!" Caitie shouted. "Don't give up! You can do it!"

It was useless, Hannah knew it was, but with both of them smiling at her expectantly, she had to go through the motions of trying one more time. She made herself trot up to the buck. This time, when she stopped, her hands on the buck, Miss Kendall and Caitie each took one of her legs and pulled her over the top. Hannah felt like a sack of cornmeal being dragged over a mountain, but there she stood, on the other side.

"Yay, Hannah!" Caitie cheered.

"Okay, Hannah, again!" Miss Kendall called out.

Hannah ran up to the buck and let herself be hoisted over a second time.

"Again!"

On her third try, Hannah gave a little more pressure with her hands and tried to get her legs up higher.

"Again!"

Hannah cleared the top easily, though she stumbled in her dismount.

"Again!"

Hannah was over, without any boost from Caitie, from Miss Kendall, from anyone.

Five times more she did her leapfrog vault, each time leaping higher. It felt almost like flying. Strains of the national anthem filled the deserted gym. A solid-gold medal was hung around her neck: Hannah Keddie, youngest gold medalist in Olympic history. . . .

"You'd better head off to lunch now, girls," Miss Kendall said, picking up her clipboard to go. Lunch? Hannah was just getting warmed up. "You did it, Hannah! Thanks to Caitie."

And she *had*.

That afternoon, she and Caitie walked to Caitie's house together, carrying their winter coats over their arms.

"Maybe the letter will come today from *The New Yorker*," Caitie said.

"Maybe," Hannah said. Anything seemed possible.

A glimpse of purple and yellow made her drop to her knees by the edge of Caitie's lawn.

"Look," she said, so happy from her triumph over the buck that she hardly cared about the mail, either way. "The first crocuses of spring."

15

The biggest math test of the marking period was set for the middle of March, on a Friday. Math didn't come easily to Hannah, as some of her other subjects did, so she had been studying hard for it all week. She had ignored Caitie's teasing and spent her lunch periods at the library, and she had insisted on going home directly after school every day, whatever fun Caitie had offered. One night she even dreamed about finding the least common denominator for a long series of dancing and singing fractions.

When she told the dream to Caitie, Caitie was amazed. "I never heard of dreaming about fractions," she said. "And I know a lot about dreams. My cousin Bonnie has this book that tells you what all your dreams mean. Like if you dream about water, that means sex."

Hannah blushed.

"I didn't make it up," Caitie said. "I'm just telling you what the book said. Or if you dream about a mad dog chasing you. That means sex, too."

"So what do you think a dream about fractions means?" Surely not *that.*

"I don't know." Caitie laughed. "It probably means that you're studying too hard."

But if Hannah was studying too hard, she knew that Caitie wasn't studying hard enough. Caitie didn't even take her math book home in her backpack at night. Hannah had a sneaking suspicion that Caitie didn't know what a least common denominator *was,* let alone how to find one.

"Maybe we should all study together for a couple of hours," Hannah suggested to Caitie as they were walking with Dawn and Samantha to Caitie's house on Thursday afternoon. Hannah had studied hard enough all week that she felt she could take a break, but she would be glad to spend the time on math instead if that would help Caitie. "I could help you study, if you wanted. You know, the way you helped me in gymnastics."

"Well, I don't need help *studying,* exactly." Caitie dropped back farther behind the others. "It's kind of too late for studying. But I was wondering . . . I mean, we sit right next to each other. If tomorrow you could sort of, you know, turn your paper a little bit? Just don't be real obvious about it, or anything."

At first Hannah was puzzled by this odd request. Then all at once she understood.

"It wouldn't really be *cheating,*" Caitie said quickly, reading the shock and disapproval on Hannah's face. "Cheating's when you copy someone's paper without asking first."

Hannah still didn't say anything. She could hardly believe that Caitie would even consider asking her to do something so dishonest and wrong.

"Or maybe it *would* be cheating, but not the bad kind. The bad kind's when you copy and then you get an A, and the other kids who didn't copy get B's and C's. But even if I got an A plus on the test, I'd still have the lowest grade for the marking period of anyone in the class. It's not wrong if you cheat just to *pass.*"

"It is, too, wrong," Hannah said. "Cheating is cheating. You know it is." She quickened her steps to catch up with the others.

"Wait, Hannah. Listen. Do you know what Dawn told me? She said that if I fail two things they can keep me back. If you don't help me, I'll fail math. I mean, I'm already failing. And I think maybe I'm going to fail science, too."

"They wouldn't make you stay back," Hannah said uncertainly. It was impossible to imagine someone as smart and grown-up as Caitie staying in fifth grade for another year.

"They'd better not," Caitie said. "But . . . well, it

would be better all around if I passed, don't you think?"

"Then why didn't you study? You haven't studied for this test at *all.*"

"Okay, I should have studied. But I didn't. And the test is tomorrow. All you have to do is just turn your paper a teeny, tiny bit. It's not cheating if someone just turns her paper *two inches.*"

Hannah knew she should tell Caitie no right then and there. But she couldn't bear the thought that Caitie might really fail and stay back. Hannah didn't want to go on to sixth grade without Caitie. It was as simple as that.

"Won't Mrs. Harding be suspicious if you get an A on the test after failing so many quizzes?"

Caitie grinned with relief. She must have sensed that Hannah was weakening. "Don't worry. I'll stick in a few wrong answers, to make it seem like it's my own work. You'll do it, Hannah? Just this once?"

Cheating was wrong, but Caitie was Hannah's friend, the best friend she had ever had. She would never have vaulted over the buck if it hadn't been for Caitie. She would never have *belonged.* Whatever her conscience said about cheating, she couldn't lose Caitie now.

"Are you coming or not, Caitie?" Dawn called from the far side of the park.

"We'll be right there!" Caitie called back.

"Okay," Hannah said slowly. "I'll do it. Just this once."

On Friday morning Mrs. Harding passed out the math

tests right after the pledge of allegiance. The test had two pages: one gave twenty problems to solve; the other was a separate answer sheet.

The problems weren't particularly hard, but Hannah felt her heart thump-thumping as she picked up her pencil to write the first answer. She was sure that Mrs. Harding could see the unusual tilt of her paper, conveniently turned toward Caitie Crystal. Hannah's fourth-grade teacher had torn up the papers of two boys she had caught cheating. Both had failed, the cheater and the cheatee.

"Let's keep our eyes to ourselves," Mrs. Harding called out. Hannah flinched, scarlet with shame. "I don't want to have to remind you again, Justin." Justin? Didn't Mrs. Harding see Caitie's sidelong glance at Hannah's exam?

One by one, Hannah worked out twenty answers and then went back to check each one, all the while keeping her answer sheet turned toward Caitie. If only Caitie had paid attention in class instead of talking. If only she had studied for just a few hours.

"All right, class, time's up! Pass your papers to the front."

Always the ham, Caitie made a pretense of checking over her paper one last time. She erased an answer, scratched her head earnestly, scribbled another in its place, erased *that* one, and then wrote in the first answer again. "Whew!" she said as she finally passed her paper forward. "That was a tough one!"

Hannah felt a surge of anger. Caitie treated cheating like a big funny joke. She had treated the Babe Ruth skit the same way. That time her clowning had gotten Hannah a B. This time it could get her an F.

Caitie kept up her act throughout the morning. "Boy, that math test was a killer!" she moaned cheerfully as the girls made their way to the cafeteria for lunch. "Problem seventeen was the worst!"

She gave Hannah just the slightest wink, but Hannah refused to laugh, or even to smile. "It's not funny," she whispered through clenched teeth.

"Oh, grow up, Hannah!" Caitie said. Her tone was light, but the words still stung.

"Excuse me," Hannah said stiffly. "I didn't know it was grown-up to be a *cheater.*"

Caitie looked angry then, too. "You didn't have to help me if you didn't want to. You know you didn't. And you don't have to be friends with me if you don't want to, either."

"I'm going to the library," Hannah said abruptly. "To *study.*"

"Fine!" Caitie said. "Dawn and I have a lot of things to talk about."

Hannah turned on her heel and left. She felt angry and hurt and, most of all, scared. Was Mrs. Harding going to find out that she and Caitie had cheated? Had her friendship with Caitie ended forever?

16

Hannah and Caitie didn't talk for the rest of the day, and after school Hannah hurried home without a word. She and her parents were going away for the weekend to visit Grandmother Keddie, who lived in the Blue Ridge Mountains down in Virginia.

Signs of spring were everywhere. Buds were beginning to appear on the redbud and dogwood trees, and forsythia bushes were laden with tiny yellow flowers. But Hannah couldn't stop thinking about the math test, and about her fight with Caitie. She almost called Caitie from Virginia to try to make things right with her again, but what could she have said? *I'm sorry I called you a cheater.* But Caitie *had* cheated and then made light of it afterward.

Yet, in spite of everything, it was hard to stay angry at Caitie. She had cheated only because she was afraid of failing. Then again, she was failing because she had refused to study. Why *didn't* Caitie study? Was it just that she was lazy? It almost seemed sometimes as if she *wanted* to fail, to keep her record as an "underachiever." Either way, Hannah shouldn't have joined her in cheating. But how could she have told her no? And now Caitie was mad at her, anyway.

However, when the Keddies pulled into their driveway Sunday night, the first thing Hannah heard was the phone ringing.

"I'll get it!" she yelled and bolted from the car. She grabbed the receiver on the fifth ring.

"Where have you been?" Caitie demanded. "I've been calling you all weekend. It's a good thing I have a phone with an automatic redial button, or my fingers would have fallen off by now."

"We went to see my grandmother," Hannah said, curious about what Caitie would say next.

"Are you still mad?" Caitie asked.

Hannah thought for a minute. "No."

"Me, neither," Caitie said.

"I'm never cheating again, though," Hannah added, and she meant it with all her heart.

"I guess I won't, either." Caitie gave a sigh. "I've been getting kind of nervous this weekend, thinking about it. Do you think Mrs. Harding's read our tests already? Maybe I should have stuck a few more wrong answers in. But what's the worst that could happen if she does find out? I'm failing, anyway, and I'd just tell her that you didn't have anything to do with it."

"But I did," Hannah said faintly. She didn't even want to think about Mrs. Harding finding out.

"Oh, well," Caitie said. "In ten years it won't matter either way, right?"

As Mrs. Harding took the pile of corrected tests from her briefcase and set them in the middle of her desk Monday morning, Hannah's mouth felt so dry she could hardly swallow. As always, Mrs. Harding handed the tests back in alphabetical order.

"Caitie Crystal."

Hannah stared straight ahead. Had Caitie gotten her B?

"Hannah Keddie."

With a rush of relief, Hannah saw that the usual big red A was marked on hers. Bolder now, she stole a glance at Caitie's desk, with her test lying on top of it in full view. The usual big red F was marked on hers.

She caught Caitie's eye. The girls stared at each other in disbelief. It didn't make sense.

As soon as the lunch bell rang and Mrs. Harding had left the room, Caitie grabbed Hannah's paper and compared it against hers. Then she burst out in merry peals of laughter.

"Look, Hannah!" She held out the two answer sheets for Hannah's inspection.

Then Hannah saw what Caitie had done. The copied answers were numbered incorrectly. Caitie had put down her own decoy wrong answer for the second question, then carelessly copied Hannah's answer two as well, which she then numbered as answer three, throwing off the entire rest of the list.

At the top of the page Mrs. Harding had written: "Random guessing is no substitute for study."

"But does this mean you'll fail?"

"Unless Mrs. Harding copies the grades wrong from her gradebook." Caitie started laughing again. "If I fail, I fail. I mean, it's only an F. It's not like they can give you a G, or an H, or a K."

"Or a P!" Hannah gave in and joined Caitie in laughter.

"Or a Z!"

It was hard not to laugh when Hannah was with Caitie. But the cheating hadn't been funny. And failing wouldn't be funny, either, not if it meant that Caitie really had to stay back a whole grade; not if it meant that Hannah had to face sixth grade alone.

"What do you think your parents are going to say?"

Caitie shrugged. "My mom's been really busy lately, teaching this special two-week seminar for doctors. You know, on the eyeball. My dad's off to a conference. I think it's in Athens. Either Athens, Georgia, or Athens, Greece. One of those places. It's not like there's a great big rush to tell them. They'll get my report card in a couple of weeks, anyway. For news like this, they can wait."

"They're gone a lot, aren't they?" Hannah hadn't

meant to sound pitying, but the question came out that way.

"I have Rita," Caitie said staunchly. "And they usually try to spend some time on the weekend with me, doing whatever I want, like going to the mall or renting a video, or something."

As if to head off any more conversation about her parents, Caitie folded her test into a paper airplane and sent it soaring toward the trash can. It missed, and Hannah picked it up for her, crumpled it into a ball, and threw it away.

17

The girls went to Caitie's house that afternoon. Downstairs in the rec room, they lay on the carpeted floor, poring over the March issue of *Seventeen* magazine.

"Look at her hair!" Dawn jeered, pointing to a picture of a model with a tangled mop of frizzy curls falling down over one eye. "Like anybody's going to go out of the house looking like that."

"I like her sweater, though," Sam said. "It'd go great with the pants my mom got me last week at the mall."

"The ones you wore on Thursday?" Caitie asked.

Sam nodded. "The top I wore with them was okay, but not super okay."

"With that shade of purple, so many things clash," Caitie said. "Your white sweater would at least be neutral. The fake angora one."

Hannah couldn't believe that the others could still

remember what Sam had worn on *Thursday.* It was as if they had memorized the contents of one another's closets. She tried to take an interest in the conversation, but the truth was that she didn't *care* what Sam had worn on Thursday, or on Wednesday, either. She didn't care which models wore which brand of jeans or which kind of ankle bracelet. Maybe she'd learn to care when she was in sixth grade, or college, or art school.

"Look at this one," Caitie said, turning the page. "Don't you think her haircut would look good on Hannah?"

Sam held the magazine up next to Hannah's head and squinted. "Uh-huh," she said.

Caitie tore out the page and handed it to Hannah. "It's good to have a picture of what you want your hair to look like when you go in for your cut."

"I'm not going in for a cut," Hannah said.

Caitie gave a mysterious smile. "But there just might be a special occasion coming up, for which you'll all want to look indescribably beauteous."

"Like what?" Dawn wanted to know.

"First let me get our frozen pizza out of the oven," Caitie said. "Don't move, anybody!"

When the girls had devoured the pizza, down to the last strings of melted mozarella cheese scraped off the paper plates, Caitie clapped her hands the way Mrs. Harding did when she wanted the class to pay attention.

"I have an announcement to make. My birthday

is on March thirty-first, and I'm going to have a party, and the whole class is invited!"

Dawn made a face. "You're inviting Lizzie Haynes? She's awfully dorky. I think her mother gets her clothes from Goodwill or something."

Hannah flushed. If she hadn't been right there, part of Caitie's charmed circle, what would Dawn have said about *her*?

Caitie gestured impatiently. "Yes, I'm inviting Lizzie. But you guys aren't listening. I said *the whole class* is invited. The *whole* class. That means—"

"Boys!" Sam said. "You're inviting boys."

Caitie paused for effect, then said: "I am."

"Roger!" Sam squealed.

"All of them."

"Justin," Dawn said thoughtfully, apparently willing now to forgive Caitie for inviting dorky girls like Lizzie—and Hannah.

"All of them. Roger for Sam and Justin for you and Brian for me and Michael for Hannah. And it's going to be at night, from seven till ten. And—well, there's more, but it's a surprise."

The *Seventeen* magazine lay forgotten on the floor. No one had had a boy-girl party since second grade. No one had ever had an evening party. And a party given by Caitie was bound to be wonderfully different from a party given by anyone else.

Hannah felt excited in spite of herself. She had been to very few parties, and those she had been to she hadn't really liked. Usually the birthday mother served a bakery sheet cake—a rectangular slab of dry yellow cake with stiff, icky-sweet frosting layered on top. The roses were the worst—hard lumps of the same frosting in horrid bright colors like canary yellow and shocking pink. "Here's a nice big piece with *two* roses on it for *you,*" the birthday mother would say to Hannah. To be polite Hannah would have to eat both, unless she could slip her plate into the trash when no one was looking.

The birthday girl opened presents, of course. Hannah thought there were few forms of torture worse than watching someone open fifteen presents, one of them yours. What if someone else gave the identical present you did? What if you gave a dumb, babyish present like a book or a doll, so that instead of oohing and ahhing the watching girls fell silent and started whispering behind their hands?

When they were younger, parties had involved games: pin-the-tail-on-the-donkey, pop-the-balloon, bobbing for apples. Hannah wasn't very good at most of them, but at least she had understood the rules and had known what was expected of her. In fourth and fifth grades, the girls had abandoned games in favor of dancing to records. Hannah hated dancing the way she hated gymnastics. She didn't really know *how* to dance, what to do with her hands, her feet, her face. So she'd slip upstairs to the kitchen to talk to the birthday girl's mother. Mothers always liked Hannah. She could just hear them saying to their daughters afterward, "Why don't you invite Hannah Keddie over to play? Such a *nice* little girl."

Now a party at night. A party with boys. A party with friends.

18

On a blustery afternoon the week before Caitie's birthday, Hannah and Caitie were walking together through the park by Caitie's house.

"What are you going to wear to my party?" Caitie asked Hannah when they stopped by the duck pond.

"I don't know. What *should* I wear?" Hannah tossed the ducks a stale bread crust from the sack Rita had given them.

"Something sophisticated," Caitie said. "Wear what you'd wear to a party in high school."

Hannah doubted that anything in her closet would qualify as sophisticated. "I don't suppose . . . well, the dress I wore to the Barbie tea party? Would that be okay?"

Caitie shook her head regretfully. "That dress says *ten*. You want a dress that says *fourteen*. I'd let you wear something of mine, but you're so much taller.

Wait! You can borrow something of Bonnie's. My cousin Bonnie. She's about your size, and she owes me a couple of favors. Anything of hers will be perfect. And if you come over early on Saturday, I'll do your makeup for you. So we're all set. Except for one thing."

Involuntarily, Hannah reached for her braid.

"You got it! Snip! Oh, Hannah, you know it's time. I mean, if you have a grown-up dress and grown-up makeup—and I'll lend you some jewelry, too—you can't have little girl hair. It'd spoil the whole effect."

"What if I put it up?" Not that Hannah had the faintest idea how such a feat would be accomplished, but maybe Caitie was as good with hair as she was with makeup. "Sort of in a bun?"

"A *bun*? The idea is to look fourteen, Hannah, not forty. No, the braid has to come off." Caitie gave a small decisive nod of her head. "I'm only telling you for your own good. What time is it?"

Hannah checked her watch. "Four o'clock."

"The Hair Place is open till six. It's just a ten-minute walk from here."

"I don't *want* to get my hair cut," Hannah said for what seemed like the dozenth time. Didn't Caitie ever *listen*?

"Look at it this way," Caitie said. "If you don't like it, you can grow it back. It's not that big a deal. It's not like a *tatoo*. It's not even like getting your ears pierced. I mean, haven't you ever thought that it would be fun to change how you look? For me getting a haircut is like getting a chance to start all over again and be somebody new and different."

"I don't want to be somebody new and different," Hannah said, but she could feel herself wavering. It did capture her imagination, put that way. Did she always want to be the same Hannah Keddie? Caitie had been talking about Hannah's haircut since that first snowy afternoon at her house. It had begun to seem impossible that Hannah *wouldn't* cut her hair.

"We don't have an appointment," Hannah pointed out.

"They have a big sign in the window: NO APPOINTMENT NEEDED."

Hannah knew that now she was just stalling for time: "I have to ask my parents at least."

"That's just what you *don't* want to do. What if they say no? Then what? They'll like it when they see it. My cousin Bonnie *dyed* her hair once. Her parents got used to it. After a while, they did."

Hannah didn't raise any other objections. Somehow she had passed the point of no return.

The girls stopped at Caitie's house to get some money, then set out for the Hair Place. The stiff March wind sent Hannah's braid streaming out behind her like the tail of a kite. For a moment her heart held fast: She couldn't cut off her braid. It was part of her. She had had her braid longer than she had had Judith. Yet she felt oddly excited, too, as she and Caitie hurried, half running, toward the beauty parlor. Hannah had never had a professional haircut before. Her father always trimmed her hair for her, scattering the clippings on the lawn for the birds in nest-building season. Whatever else it was, this was undeniably an adventure.

Once inside the Hair Place, Caitie did all the talking.

"My friend wants a haircut," she told the receptionist.

"Just a trim?"

Caitie shook her head. "She wants it short. My length."

The receptionist measured Hannah's braid with her eyes. "There's no point washing all that. Let's take off the excess length first, before we send you back to shampoo."

"But—" Hannah clamped her lips shut. How could she explain that she needed time to say good-bye to her braid? She wanted to shake out her long crinkly hair one last time and then plait it up again, weaving the three long strands back and forth with the quick, effortless motions that were so familiar to her fingers. She needed a little more *time*.

The receptionist gave her a suspicious look. "Now, your mother knows about this, doesn't she?"

Not exactly. It was the moment to cry out, the last chance to save her braid from the executioner's blade.

"Oh, yes," Caitie answered for her. "It was her

mother's idea. She thought short hair would make her look, you know, more grown-up.''

Mutely Hannah nodded.

Six big padded swivel chairs stood in a row in front of an enormous mirror. The receptionist sent Hannah over to the third one. A pretty young woman dressed in jeans and a man's striped shirt picked up a pair of long scissors and smiled pleasantly at Hannah.

''I'm Tiffany,'' she introduced herself. ''So you're going to take the plunge.''

Again Hannah made herself nod. She felt like a daredevil in a barrel, about to be shoved over the top of Niagara Falls.

''Here goes!''

Hannah reached for Caitie's hand. *Good-bye, braid, good-bye!*

Snip! In one brief, fatal moment, the deed was done. Hannah's braid lay lifeless on the floor, a pink bow still tied to the end of it. It was hard to believe that it couldn't be undone just as easily. *Put it back,* Hannah wanted to say. *I changed my mind.* But the braid couldn't be snapped back onto her head like the detachable hood on a raincoat.

''Okay, hon, let's get your hair shampooed and then we'll give you a real pretty cut.''

Hannah hardly noticed as her hair was shampooed and rinsed and combed out tangle free. Then: Snip! Snip! Tiffany kept the scissors clipping, close to Hannah's head. Snip! Snip! But a hundred of these snips didn't equal that first terrible one, the one that had ended Hannah's life as Little Girl with Braid.

Now Tiffany was blow-drying Hannah's hair. Hannah still hadn't stolen a glance in the mirror.

"Okay, hon, what do you think?"

Dreading what she might see, Hannah focused her eyes on her reflection in the glass. But she looked pretty. She looked like Caitie and Dawn and Sam. It was as if Tiffany had copied the haircut out of *The Popular Girls' Book of Opinions about Everything,* from the chapter on haircuts.

"Ooh, Hannah!" Caitie pretended to swoon at the beauty of the sight. "Wait till everyone sees you in school tomorrow. Wait till *Michael* sees you!"

"I'll wrap this up for you to take home." Tiffany stooped down to pick up something from the floor—Hannah's braid.

"Just leave it," Hannah said. Suddenly the lump of unshed tears in her throat rose up to choke her. She swallowed hard.

Caitie paid the bill and took care of the tip.

"Take it," Tiffany said, pressing a small paper bag into Hannah's hand. "Your mom may want it."

Hannah didn't cry. She was too old to cry. She took the bag and with Caitie beside her walked out into the chilly gray afternoon.

19

"You *do* like it, don't you?" Caitie asked a block later.

"I don't know," Hannah said. She honestly didn't. She mourned her lost braid with mingled guilt and longing. But her head felt wonderfully light and airy. The wind playfully tickled her unprotected ears. She felt bold and brave, afraid of nothing. If there had been a buck handy, she would have vaulted over it a few dozen times for good measure.

"You will," Caitie predicted confidently. "What do you think your parents will say?"

Abruptly Hannah's bold, brave feeling vanished. What *would* her parents say?

"It's your hair," Caitie said, as if fortifying Hannah with arguments she might need later. "What a person does with her own hair is her own business. It's a free country, right?"

Hannah clutched Tiffany's paper bag more

tightly. Maybe she could fasten the braid back on somehow, just temporarily. At least until she could prepare her parents a little bit. She wasn't sure exactly why she dreaded their reaction. It wasn't as if they had ever said, "Now, whatever you do, Hannah, don't cut your hair." It was more the way her father would give a gentle tug to her braid as she lay on the couch sketching. Or how her mother would sit patiently for fifteen minutes at a stretch combing out tangles.

Back at Caitie's, Hannah let Caitie steer her into the kitchen, where Rita was peeling potatoes for the Crystals' dinner.

"Ta-dah! Don't you love it?"

"Very pretty!" Rita said admiringly, wiping her wet hands on her apron. "So trim and smart-looking! Just right for spring."

Hannah's hopes rose. Maybe her mother would look up from the four o'clock movie and say, "Just right for spring." But in the car on the way home, Hannah thought instead about ways to postpone the moment of discovery. Could she invent some reason to wear a scarf on her head for the next three or four years? If only she could come down with brain fever at the next traffic light and have to have her head shaved entirely.

Rita pulled into the Keddies' driveway. "Do you want me to come in with you?" Caitie asked. "I could help explain, you know, tell them that it was all my idea and everything."

"That's okay," Hannah said. She went in alone.

Her father saw her first. "Hanniken!" he called as she tried to slip past the living room door. "Come here! I have something to show you."

Unwillingly, Hannah presented herself in the doorway.

"I found it in the back meadow when I was out tramping around this afternoon. Pussy willow. Another sign of spring for your list."

Then he looked up, looked straight at her. At first he didn't seem to understand.

"Your hair. You did something to it."

"I got it cut."

"So I see. Susan!" he bellowed. "Susan, I think you'd better come out here for a minute."

"Are you mad?" Hannah asked him.

"I don't know," he said. He didn't look mad, just sad, but somehow the sadness was worse than anger would have been. "I guess I've never understood why somebody would want to look like everybody else. You look like Caitie now—which I take it is supposed to be the point of this? What was wrong with looking like Hannah?"

Hannah's mother came in from the dining room. "What's the matter?" Then: "Oh, Hannah, your braid! That beautiful, beautiful hair! It'll take you years to grow it back. Years!" Hannah was used to seeing her mother cry over movies, but this was different. It was real, for one thing, and there wasn't any pleasure in it.

Her father's sad look and her mother's tears made Hannah feel terrible, yet all at once defiant, too.

"I don't want to grow it back!" She was surprised to find herself almost shouting. "I'm tired of looking like a baby and having dolls and no friends and being years and years behind everyone else. You can't stop me from growing up! You can't!"

Hannah's mother was hugging her now, holding her close and stroking her short-cropped hair. Hannah's father looked distinctly uncomfortable. He hated it when the women in his family cried. His taste in movies was different from his wife's. He liked to watch musicals and shoot-'em-up westerns.

"So that's what this is all about," he said. "Growing up. Couldn't you just have put your hair up in a bun or something?"

"A *bun*? The idea is to look fourteen, Daddy, not forty."

"Fourteen," Hannah's father said. "What happened to ten and a half?"

"What did—what did they do with it?" her mother asked.

"With my braid? Here it is." Hannah held out the crumpled paper bag that she had been clutching for the past hour.

"Oh, Hannah!" Her mother started crying all over again.

"Oh, Mom!" Hannah was crying, too.

"Oh, Hildegarde!" Hannah's father said to the

cat, dozing next to the tea things like a large marmalade-colored tea cozy.

So it was going to be all right. Hannah's parents still loved her, even with her braid in a bag. But that night, in bed, holding Judith close under the covers, Hannah knew that she was growing apart from her parents, growing toward a different future and leaving them behind. The snow-day afternoon seemed far away and long ago, and Hannah felt her heart breaking for what was gone forever.

20

When Hannah went to brush her hair the next morning, her hair *stopped* partway through the first stroke, and the brush kept on going. It was an odd sensation. She wondered how long it would take to teach her hand a different habit of brushing, after so many years of long hair.

As she got dressed, she was surprised each time she caught a glimpse in the mirror of a pretty short-haired stranger. She found she missed doing things with her braid—flipping it over her shoulder, twirling the end of it, retying its bow. What did people without braids do with their hands? What did they clutch when they were anxious or sad?

"You got your hair cut," Mrs. Hanson, the school-bus driver, said when Hannah climbed on board. "It looks cute."

"You got your hair cut," two other girls on the bus told her—as if she didn't know.

Hannah steeled herself to walk across the playground behind Greenwood Park School. Sure enough, her new look created a sensation among both the fifth-grade boys and girls.

"Hannah got her hair cut! Hannah got her hair cut!" Brian chanted.

"Oh, *Hannah*!" Samantha moaned with delight. "I *love* it! It's *you,* Hannah, it really is!"

Even Dawn gave a grudging nod of approval. *It was about time you cut off that dumb braid,* her look said. Caitie stood by, beaming, as if she herself had clipped every strand.

Michael hadn't yet said anything about Hannah's hair. Hannah couldn't help being curious about his reaction, but when she glanced his way, he was looking down at the ground, his hands jammed in his pockets.

He stopped by her desk as they took their seats. "What happened to your hair?" he asked.

"I got it cut."

"It was real pretty before," was all he said.

Hannah felt miffed—who was Michael Malone to have opinions about her hair?—and a little sad, too. Maybe all along it had been her braid, and not its owner, that had had a secret admirer. Or maybe Michael was like her father: Maybe he had liked Hannah because she looked different from the others and was disappointed now that she looked just the same.

Mrs. Harding commented on Hannah's haircut. Mrs. Tomacki did a double take when she passed Hannah in the hall. The ladies in the cafeteria line each had something to say. Hannah half expected that her haircut would make the six o'clock news. But if she was going to be a star for a day, she wished it were for something other than a new hairstyle. If only everyone were congratulating her instead on the publication of one of her pictures on the cover of a famous national magazine. . . . But that was one dream that apparently wasn't going to come true.

The third-quarter report cards were issued on that Friday, the day before Caitie's birthday. For the first time in her life, Hannah's stomach knotted as Mrs. Harding handed out the familiar brown envelopes just before the closing bell. She wasn't worried about her own grades—she knew she'd get her usual A's, marred by the C she had come to expect in gym. But now she had Caitie's report card to think about, as well. Would Caitie get an F in math? In science, too? Even her work in social studies had been shaky.

"I'd like to see you after class, please, Caitie," Mrs. Harding said in a low voice when she handed the card to her. That didn't sound good. Caitie took her report card, but didn't open it. It was like Caitie not to give Mrs. Harding the satisfaction of thinking she cared.

Hannah opened hers. It had three surprises in it. The first was a B in art. Mrs. McCloskey had given Hannah a failing grade on the Clorox bottle piggy bank, which brought down her overall average. Hannah tried not to mind. A grade in Intermediate Clorox Bottles wasn't the same as a grade in a real art class, and at least she had done well in language arts, despite the Babe Ruth B. The second surprise was an A in gym. An A! Apparently Miss Kendall had graded heavily for effort, but still, an A! In the space on the back for overall comments Mrs. Harding had written, "Hannah continues to be a delight, though occasionally I have had to reprimand her for talking." That was the third surprise. In trouble for talking!

The bell rang. Caitie sauntered up to Mrs. Harding's desk, her report card still unopened. Hannah, Dawn, and Samantha waited for her outside in the hall.

"She's going to be kept back," Dawn said. She sounded almost pleased at the prospect of her dire prediction coming true.

"Her parents'll just send her someplace else," Sam said. "Some other private school. They have piles of money."

Hannah's throat was dry. She didn't want Caitie to go someplace else.

"I don't think another school would take her," Dawn said. "It's not like this is the first place she's flunked out of."

"But she's so smart!" Hannah burst out. "How can she be failing?"

"Smart isn't everything," Dawn said. "She doesn't do the work. That's all there is to it."

119

But Hannah knew there was more to it than that. She remembered Caitie almost bragging about how her grades drove her parents crazy. Caitie's parents were so busy, with their medical work and their writing and their constant travel. Maybe her poor performance in school was Caitie's way of trying to get her parents' attention, of trying to make them care.

"Wait, here she comes," Sam announced.

Caitie wasn't crying, but she had a bright spot of red in each cheek. "Let's go," she said.

"Soooo?" Dawn demanded. "What happened?"

"You know," Caitie said. "The same old stuff. I'm not working up to my potential. Blah blah blah. If my grades don't improve, blah blah blah."

Dawn pounced on that. "If your grades don't improve, *what*?"

"You know. They'll keep me back."

See? Dawn's triumphant look seemed to say. "Oh, Caitie, that's *terrible*!" she gushed.

"Well, it hasn't happened yet," Caitie said, but she didn't sound as confident as she had in the past. "I have two and a half months to bring up my grades. How hard can it be to get a few A's and B's? I mean, even *boys* get B's."

But it was hard, Hannah knew. She spent several hours every day on homework, and more on the weekend, even when she'd rather be out walking or painting. She had given up a lot of lunches with Caitie and after-school socializing. Good grades meant steady, sustained study, day after day after day. Hannah didn't know if Caitie was capable of working like that. But she'd do whatever she could to help her, if Caitie would let her.

"What will your parents say?" Hannah asked casually.

"I'm not going to show it to them until Sunday," Caitie said. "Till after the party."

"Mine grab my report card the minute I walk in the door," Sam said. "They write REPORT CARD DAY in big red letters on the kitchen calendar."

"Well, mine don't," Caitie said. She shoved her report card into her backpack. Hannah saw that Caitie's pack still didn't have any textbooks in it, just a jumble of lipsticks and scarves and compacts. "Okay, you guys, it's countdown to party time! And don't forget, there's going to be a surprise at the party."

"What kind of surprise?" Sam wanted to know.

"Wait and see," Caitie said, tossing back a falling bang. "Wait and see."

But to Hannah, when the others were out of earshot, she whispered hotly, "I'm not staying in fifth grade another year, and I'm not changing schools again, either. I'm not! And they can't make me!"

21

The dress lay on Caitie's bed in all its splendor. It was black velvet, with a softly gathered skirt and tiny, tight-fitting bodice. The bodice stopped right above where breasts would be, if the person wearing the dress had any—a little skimpy, skinny tube with no sleeves, no straps, no *anything.*

"I'm supposed to wear this?" Hannah asked.

"I hope, I hope, I hope it fits," Caitie said. "Quick, try it on."

Too stunned to protest, Hannah shed her Indian-print skirt and leotard and let Caitie zip her into Bonnie's party dress.

Caitie sighed with rapture. "It's perfect, Hannah. None of my Barbies has a dress as terrific as this. The boys will faint. We'd better call the rescue squad right now and have them station an ambulance outside the house."

Hannah looked in Caitie's mirror at the tall slim

girl with the bare white shoulders. It was hard to imagine her with a fat braid hanging over one of them.

"Shoes!" Caitie said. "We forgot about shoes."

Hannah looked down. Sure enough, her brown loafers spoiled the effect of the borrowed finery.

"You'll have to wear a pair of mine. What size are you?"

"Six."

"I'm a five. Well, it's only for one evening."

As Hannah wedged her feet into a pair of Caitie's shiny black sling-back shoes, Caitie changed into her own party clothes: dressy black pants topped by a gold-sequined sweater. The sweater was made so that one shoulder was covered and the other was bare.

"You look beautiful," Hannah told her.

And she did. But Hannah couldn't help noticing that Caitie was uncharacteristically quiet as she rifled through her jewelry box and tried on earrings. Was she still worried about her report card? And where was Caitie's mother? Hannah had never met either of Caitie's parents; she was looking forward to seeing them preside over the party. You'd think Caitie's mother would be upstairs with her now, sitting at the foot of the bed, giving her advice about her jewelry and hair. Not that Hannah's mother could have given advice about jewelry or hair to save her life. But if the party were at Hannah's house, at least her mother would be at the door, greeting her friends and making them feel welcome. She would *be* there.

"I have some bad news," Caitie said abruptly.

Hannah had a sinking feeling that Caitie was going to say, *My mother's away, on my birthday.*

"Do you want me to tell you now? I was going to wait until after the party, but maybe the party will cheer you up, and I kind of have some good news, too."

"Now," Hannah said, puzzled.

Caitie handed Hannah a large brown envelope, addressed to Caitie Crystal. What kind of bad news came in large brown envelopes? Then she saw the return address: The envelope was from *The New Yorker.*

Hannah had known all along that the magazine wouldn't want her drawing. She had tried never to let herself hope. Yet as she took the envelope with her poor little picture inside, she realized that she *had* hoped, after all. Hannah had found herself stealing glances at copies of *The New Yorker* on Caitie's coffee table, imagining Hildegarde on the cover. A quick surge of tears stung her eyes. She should have learned her lesson the last time. She should have known better than to think anyone would want to publish her pictures.

"Read the letter. It's nice."

Hannah made no move to open the envelope.

"Read it," Caitie said again.

So Hannah did. The letter was typed on fancy

stationery, with the name and address of the magazine printed on top.

Miss Caitlin Crystal
2734 Parkside Lane
Greenwood Park, MD 20950

Dear Miss Crystal:

We are returning your client's drawing to you, with regret. We agree that she is very talented, but it is difficult for even the most gifted young artist to compete with adult professionals.

Please tell Miss Keddie that we look forward to seeing her work again in a few years.

> *Sincerely,*
> *Alison Andrews*
> *Editorial Assistant*

"See? She said you were very talented. And most gifted. And that you'd grow up to be an artist."

Hannah stuffed the letter back into the envelope, roughly. "What else was she going to say? She was just being *nice.* Let's not talk about it anymore, okay? You said you had some good news, too."

"Well, I found another place you can send your picture. When one place doesn't want it, you send it somewhere else right away. That's what my father learned when he did his heart attack book. It was rejected nine times before his agent found him a publisher. Anyway, there's a contest, an art contest, for kids. It's for the whole county, and you compete against other kids in your grade. You know, to make it fair."

"I already know all about it," Hannah said wearily. Mrs. Tomacki had told her last week that there were just a few days left to enter.

"Doesn't it sound perfect? Rita made me go to the library this morning, and I saw a flyer for it on a bulletin board there. I copied down the stuff you need to know. I have it here somewhere. Wait! Here it is."

Caitie fished out a soiled scrap of paper from the pocket of the jeans lying on the floor next to her bed. Mechanically, Hannah tucked it into the bottom of one of her loafers. This was Caitie's good news? Hannah wasn't sending her pictures anywhere, ever again. She wasn't going to let Caitie raise her hopes only to have them dashed one more time.

As in the first week of their friendship, Caitie put mascara and lipstick on Hannah. Hannah felt too discouraged about the *New Yorker* rejection to try to stop her. Caitie's own makeup was heavier than Hannah had seen her wear before. She had a smudge of pale green eye shadow over each eye, and her cheeks were pink with blush-on.

"There!" Caitie said, surveying herself in the mirror, side by side with Hannah. "The rescue squad better have extra staff on tonight!"

"I thought your mother didn't let you wear so much makeup," Hannah ventured.

"She's not here," Caitie said brightly. "Or my father, either. Just Rita. There was a mix-up, and it turned out that this was a weekend they had to be away."

"Oh, Caitie!"

"It *happens.*" Caitie's tone was almost sharp. "I mean, when people are busy and important, they can't always be where they want to be. It's okay. This way I can do whatever I want. I can wear makeup two inches thick if I feel like it. There's no one to care."

No one to care. It didn't sound all that wonderful to Hannah.

The doorbell rang.

"The guests are arriving!" Caitie said, grabbing Hannah's hand and squeezing it hard. "The party of the century has begun!"

22

At first it was as if there were two different parties going on in Caitie's basement at the same time. The girls stood on one side of the room admiring one another's fancy party dresses and shoes and jewelry and barrettes. The boys, wearing regular school clothes, jostled one another around the pool table, playing successive games of eight-ball. The two groups met only at the refreshment table, where Rita had set up the fixings for make-your-own tacos.

Then the lights dimmed, and Rita carried in the cake, its eleven candles flickering in the draft from the stairwell. "Happy birthday to you," everybody sang, the boys too awed by the splendor of Caitie's house to add the obligatory second verse about how Caitie lived in a zoo, looked like a monkey, and was one, too. Caitie managed to blow out all the candles in one try, which meant her wish would come true. Hannah didn't know what Caitie had wished for, but she made her own wish as the candles whooshed out: *Let Caitie and me stay friends forever.*

The cake was delicious: a rich dark chocolate mousse cake, served with scoops of gourmet vanilla ice cream.

"You'd better start opening presents," Dawn told Caitie. "It's eight-thirty already, and you have the boys' presents to open, too."

"I'm not going to open them tonight. It's boring to watch someone open presents."

"But I want to know what Roger gave you," Sam said.

"You guys can come over and open them with me tomorrow," Caitie promised.

Hannah was relieved, even though she thought Caitie would like the present she had chosen: her picture of Caitie, finished now and carefully matted and framed. Caitie liked Hannah's pictures, even if nobody else did.

Hannah shifted her weight to her left foot and slipped her right foot out of its tight, hot prison. Her feet were on fire. Now Hannah could identify with Cinderella's wicked stepsisters, their oversized feet shoved into the dainty glass slipper.

"Come on, everybody! Boys, too!" Caitie called. "Sit here in a circle. It's time for a game."

Thankfully, Hannah eased off Caitie's shoes and sank to the floor. It was a pleasant surprise that Caitie was still having games at her party. Hannah had assumed that grown-up Caitie would automatically opt for dancing to records, made more exciting by the availability of boys as partners. It was nice to think that they weren't too old for one last round of "Who am I?" with names of famous people pinned to their backs, or "How many items on this tray can you memorize in ten seconds?" Those were the two games Hannah was best at, and they both started with everybody in a circle.

"Okay," Caitie said when even the boys had found their places. Mischief gleamed in her eyes. From behind her back she produced an empty Pepsi bottle.

"Oh, *Caitie,*" Sam squealed, covering her face coyly with both hands. Dawn smiled smugly, but most of the others looked perplexed. Certainly Hannah couldn't remember any party game played with empty soft-drink bottles.

"Spin-the-bottle," Caitie announced. "When you're 'it,' you spin the bottle, and whoever it points to, you have to kiss."

"No way!" "Oh, Caitie, that's awful!" "Forget it!" "My mother won't let me!" "Of all the dumb games girls think of!" "Yuck!" "No way, José!"

But despite the chorus of protests, nobody moved out of the circle.

"*If* it's a member of the opposite sex," Caitie continued when everyone was quiet again. "If the bottle points to a member of the same sex, you have to spin again."

Hannah sat silent in the shadow cast by the basement wet bar. If she could have slipped upstairs unnoticed, she would have, but Caitie was closest to the door. And the game undeniably had its fascinations. Would Sam spin to Roger? Brian to Caitie? And what about Michael? Fervently Hannah prayed that spin-the-bottle would be like gym class softball, over before her turn would ever come.

"Who wants to go first?" Caitie asked, holding out the bottle. The kids sitting closest to her shrank back as if it were a ticking time bomb. "No volunteers? Okay, *I'll* spin."

Caitie stepped into the middle of the circle. She knelt down, laid the bottle on its side, and spun. When it stopped, the bottle was pointing to Lizzie Haynes.

"So I spin again."

Round it went, once, twice, then—

"Justin!" everybody shouted.

Caitie scooted over to Justin and gave him a kiss on his beet-red cheek. Hannah thought Dawn looked relieved that Caitie hadn't kissed him on the lips.

"Now *you're* 'it.' " Caitie handed the bottle to Justin. He spun to Molly Davis and gave her the kind of quick peck you'd give to an elderly maiden aunt. Molly spun to one of the other boys. He spun to Sam, who spun to—Roger! How she had made it happen,

Hannah didn't know, but there was no mistaking it. The bottle pointed directly at Roger, sitting in front of the large-screen TV.

Sam went over to Roger and moved in for the kiss. It was obvious that she did not intend to kiss Roger on the cheek. But in the nick of time Roger turned his head, and the kiss landed harmlessly somewhere in the vicinity of his ear.

Roger spun to Heather Marshall. Heather spun to Michael. Each time the bottle whirled around, Hannah's heart skipped a beat: *Please, please, please don't let it be me.*

Michael spun.

"It's Evan," someone said.

"No, it's more toward Hannah," Caitie insisted. *"Han*-nah!"

Hannah closed her eyes as Michael moved toward her, steeling herself for the moment when his lips would graze her cheek. But Michael didn't kiss Hannah's cheek. He kissed her full on the mouth.

It wasn't a long kiss, the way lovers kissed on Hannah's mother's tear-jerking movies. But it was a real kiss, the first of the evening—the first of Hannah's life.

"Oooh, Hannah!" the girls shrieked.

"Way to go, *Michael*!" one of the boys hollered.

"Hannah and Michael sitting in a tree, K-I-S-S-I-N-G," someone else started singing.

"Now it's your turn, Hannah," Caitie said. "Spin."

"Maybe you'll get *Michael*!" "First comes love, then comes marriage. . . ." "Spin, Hannah, spin!"

Hannah stood up unsteadily on her swollen, aching feet. "I don't want to play," she said. To her horror, she felt wet tears sliding down her cheeks.

"*Han*-nah! Come on, you have to play." This, from Caitie.

"Oh, let her go," Dawn said, her voice too loud in the sudden silence that had fallen over the group. "I told you all along she was a big baby, Caitie. I mean, you're the one who told me she still plays with *dolls.*"

"Hannah kisses do-olls," Justin sang out, laughing. "Hannah kisses do-olls."

So Caitie had betrayed her, after all. Slowly, without daring to look at Michael, Hannah walked through the circle of players and up the basement stairs, and the sound of their laughter followed her.

23

Laughter, and then Caitie's quick light footsteps behind her.

"Hannah! I'm sorry, I really am. I didn't mean—"

In the kitchen now, Hannah whirled to face her. "You told her. About the tea party. About everything. The two of you together, laughing at me!"

"It wasn't like that. It *wasn't*. Or maybe it was, but you never said not to tell. You didn't make it like a great big secret or anything. And I wouldn't have told Dawn except—well, it was the day we did the math test, and you were acting so goody-goody about it, and I was mad. But I *liked* the Barbie party. You know I did. I *loved* it. I mean, they were *my* Barbies. I was there, too. I played with dolls, too. And I was sorry I told Dawn afterward. I don't even like Dawn, not really. It's just that she was the first person who acted friendly to me after I changed schools, and so I was friendly back, and when you're friends with somebody sometimes you tell them things and then you wish you hadn't. Hannah, you have to understand."

"No, I don't." Hannah turned and ran up the second flight of stairs to Caitie's room. The first thing she had to do was to change her clothes, to stop looking like Bonnie and Caitie and Dawn and start looking like Hannah again. She yanked at the zipper on Bonnie's dress.

"I'll do it," Caitie said, closing the door behind them.

Hannah stood still and let Caitie unzip her. Neither girl spoke as Hannah laid Bonnie's dress back on the bed and slipped into her own unfashionable, comfortable clothes.

"The stuff on my face. The *makeup.*" Hannah spat it out like a dirty word. "I want to take it off."

"Here," Caitie said. "Cold cream is best." She seated Hannah at the vanity table and handed her a box of tissues and a jar of cleansing cream.

With a few brisk wipes, the sooty black on Hannah's eyelashes was gone, and the Wild Strawberry on her lips, and the dusting of blush-on on her cheeks.

"But my braid. I can't put *that* back on, can I?"

"Hannah!" Through the blinding haze of her anger, Hannah dimly realized that Caitie was crying. "I thought you wanted . . . I thought . . . I was just trying to *help.* I mean, growing up is hard if you don't have anyone to help. And I have Bonnie, and I could tell you didn't have . . . Well, you said your mother

135

wasn't . . . Oh, Hannah, hasn't any of it been fun? You looked so pretty tonight. That's why Michael—" Caitie faltered then. "You just *did.*"

Hannah tried to hold on to the cold certainty of her anger against Caitie. "You never liked me. You just wanted to change me, to make me over into someone just like you and Sam and Dawn. Somebody *grown up.* Somebody who looks like you and dresses like you and talks like you. Why does everybody have to grow up at the same time? Can't you see that some people just aren't *ready* to grow up? Like me. I'm not *ready.* I *do* play with dolls. I *love* my dolls. I would *never* put them in a box just because of you or Dawn."

"I don't *want* you to. I don't!"

"Do you know what I got from the library this week? To read? Not for a book report, just for me. Do you want to know? *The Blue Fairy Book.* I'm not *ready* for *Seventeen* magazine. I want *Ten* magazine, *Nine* even. I'm not ready for makeup or party dresses with no straps on them or kissing boys. I'll never be ready for *cheating.* And I didn't want to send my stupid picture of a stupid cat to a stupid magazine, either. Come back when you grow up, that's what they said. Well, I'm going to take my time growing up. I am!"

"Caitie!" It was Rita's voice, wafting up the stairs. "Are you up there? Your mama's here!"

"But she wasn't coming back till tomorrow," Caitie said, as if to herself. Then her face lit up with gladness. "Oh, Hannah, she *did* come."

"Caitie? Are you there?" It was Dr. Crystal's voice this time, girlish sounding for somebody's mother.

"Coming!"

Caitie hugged Hannah, hard, and then turned and raced down the stairs.

Hannah couldn't help herself: She crept to the top of the stairs and watched from the shadowy hall above. She saw Caitie's mother waiting in the foyer—petite like Caitie, with the same short dark hair and delicate pointed chin. Dr. Crystal was wearing a stylish suit, not a white doctor's coat. Right then she didn't look particularly like a doctor at all. She looked like . . . well, just like Caitie's mother.

"Mom!" Caitie flung herself into her mother's arms.

"Oh, Caitie!" Hannah heard Dr. Crystal say. "I decided to cancel everything and come back early. I've been away so much this spring, I couldn't miss your birthday. Are you all right?" She held Caitie out at arm's length and looked at her. "You've been crying! Your mascara is all streaked. Honey, I thought I told you not to wear so much makeup. You're only eleven, you know."

"I'll wash it off," Caitie offered cheerfully. "I'll go scrub it all off right now if you want."

"But why were you crying?" her mother asked again.

"I just was," Caitie said. "I'll tell you tomorrow.

And, um, there's some other stuff we have to talk about then, too." Hannah knew that Caitie was thinking about her report card. "You *will* be here tomorrow, won't you?"

Dr. Crystal took a tissue from her purse and dabbed at Caitie's damp face. "All day long," she promised. It didn't sound like very long to Hannah, but Caitie looked pleased. "Now, go on back to your party."

Hannah saw Caitie hesitate, remembering their quarrel.

"Go on, honey. Your guests will be wondering where you've been."

"In a minute. I just need one minute. There's something I have to tell somebody."

Caitie tore herself free from her mother and ran up the stairs, almost colliding with Hannah at the top.

"I do like you," she said fiercely. "You're my best friend, and I love you, just exactly the way you are. Maybe I did try to change you, but I'll never do it ever again. I won't. Really truly, I won't. All I want is for us to be friends again. Okay?"

Hannah didn't know if she wanted to be friends anymore with Caitie or not. Friendship was too hard. Sometimes it hurt too much. But there was no way she could find the words to say all that she was feeling, not with Caitie's mother waiting right below.

Half crying, she hugged Caitie back. Then Caitie ran downstairs again.

24

Hannah slept late the next morning, till half past eight. She didn't want to get up, to throw back the quilts and put one bare foot and then the other down on the bleached white floorboards. She lay absolutely still and motionless, breathing as slowly as she could: in, out, in, out. She pretended that she could stop time that way, or at least slow its pace: If she breathed slowly enough, maybe she could make time run backward, so that it would still be Saturday, with Caitie's party yet to come. If only she could make it that Caitie's party had never happened. Or that it was still that snowy morning in January, the day before she and Caitie first became friends.

No. If Hannah had a big enough pink rubber eraser, she'd rub out the party, but not the friendship. She had been mad at Caitie last night, but her wish on Caitie's birthday candles still held: She didn't want to go back to life before Caitie. *Hasn't any of it been fun?*

Caitie had asked her. If Hannah was being honest, she'd have to answer that most of it had been wonderful: laughing together outside Mr. Blake's office, having the Barbie tea party, sharing her valentine from a secret admirer, soaring over the buck. Hannah had done things she never thought she'd do: some good, some bad, some scary, some glorious.

There was a gentle tap on Hannah's door. Then her mother nudged the door open. She was carrying a wooden tray with breakfast on it.

"May I come in, Hannah, love? I brought you some cinnamon-apple muffins and a pot of hot chocolate."

Hannah slid over to make room for her mother at the edge of the bed. She knew her mother realized something had gone wrong at the party. During the ride home, Hannah had kept her head turned away to hide the stray tears that still spilled over. But her mother must have noticed: She had reached over at one traffic light and hugged Hannah's shoulders, without prying.

"Do you want to tell me about the party?" her mother asked now. The hot chocolate was in a stout ceramic pitcher, one of Hannah's favorites. Her mother poured from it into a matching cup.

Hannah took a small sip. It had been a long time since she had confided in her mother.

"It's just that—well, Caitie and her friends are so grown up. And I'm not. And I don't *want* to be."

Haltingly, she told her mother everything, about Bonnie's dress, and Caitie's makeup, and the terrible moment when she had fled from the room after Michael's kiss. When she had finished, the hot chocolate in her cup was as cool as chocolate milk. She drained the last of it in a single gulp.

"Oh, Hannah," her mother said, reaching over the quilts to take her hand. "Where did you ever get the idea that growing up has to do with haircuts and makeup and clothes and spin-the-bottle? I'm forty-three years old and about as grown up as I'm going to be, and I still don't know a thing about the new spring hairstyles or how to wear makeup so that it looks like you're not wearing makeup, or how to 'dress for success.' And it's been thirty years since I've played a kissing game at a party."

Hannah took a bite of muffin. "But Caitie just *seems* so grown up. Doesn't she to you?"

"In some ways, yes. She's grown up enough not to be overly impressed by girls like Dawn. She sounds like a leader, not a follower. She's grown up enough to value having someone like you as a friend—and that counts for a lot in my book! But I think Caitie's too concerned with what she thinks are the outward signs of maturity—the clothes, the jewelry, and all that. And I think if Caitie were more grown up, she'd realize that what she loves about you as a friend is precisely the ways in which you're different from her. Caitie doesn't need another Caitie to be friends with; she needs a

Hannah. She needs you, just the way you are."

It was almost what Caitie had said herself the night before.

"Even though I still like dolls and fairy tales."

"*Because* you do. Listen, Hannah, you may still have a doll family when you're forty. I still lie on the couch crying over movies. It doesn't make me any less grown up than other people who never cry at anything."

Hannah picked up Judith, who had been lying face down in the covers, and retied the blue ribbon in her soft curly hair.

Her mother stood up and took the breakfast tray. "It's going to be in the seventies today. Hurry up and get dressed, and I'll talk your father into a hike on Sugarloaf Mountain."

Alone again, Hannah quickly changed out of her nightgown and into her dungarees and a worn flannel shirt. She shoved her feet into her old loafers, but something in the toe of one of them didn't feel right. Of course: It was the slip of paper Caitie had given her with the art contest information scribbled on it. She had been too miserable to bother throwing it away the night before.

Now she crumpled it into a tiny wad and tossed it into the wastepaper basket beside her drawing table. But then, slowly, she stooped down and took it out again. Caitie had gone to a lot of trouble to copy all that information from the bulletin board. Caitie had believed in Hannah's talent even when Hannah hadn't. Mrs. Tomacki had, too. Hannah owed it to both of them to try one more time.

Hannah smoothed out the paper and read Caitie's notes over twice, then a third time. She didn't just owe it to her friends to try again. She owed it to herself. The most grown-up thing she had done since knowing Caitie wasn't cutting her hair or letting a boy kiss her; it was making herself vault over the buck. "Again!" Miss Kendall had shouted. "Don't give up!" Caitie had hollered. "You can do it!" And Hannah *had* done it. She really had.

Growing up means trying again and again, and not giving up. Growing up means doing something you've never done before—something you're afraid to do, that you don't know how to do—and doing it, anyway.

Like friendship, Hannah thought suddenly. She had never had a real friend before Caitie. Friendship had turned out to be harder than she had thought anything could be. She had been so mad at Caitie sometimes, and Caitie had been just as angry at her. They were so different, and it wasn't always easy accepting that. But when they quarreled, they made up again. They didn't give up on each other. Through everything, they were still friends.

Still in her stocking feet, Hannah slipped the Hildegarde drawing out of its brown *New Yorker* envelope. She pretended that she was seeing it for the first time, the way the editors at *The New Yorker* had seen it, the way the judges would see it in the countywide art contest. It *was* good. But one paw in front was too large, and Hannah could see now that there wasn't enough contrast between Hildegarde and the window behind her. And there was something about the light. . . . The picture was good, but it could be better. Hannah was going to make it better, and then she'd send it to the art contest. She wouldn't give up. She wasn't grown up yet, but she was on her way.

Suddenly she thought about Caitie's report card. Today was the day Caitie was showing it to her mother and telling her mother that she might have to stay back in fifth grade. Despite the things Hannah's mother had said, Caitie was still the most grown-up fifth grader Hannah knew. However, there was nothing grown up about having to stay in fifth grade when everybody else went on to sixth.

Right then Hannah made a vow to herself. Caitie had helped her get over the buck; she'd help Caitie get through fifth grade in exactly the same way. They'd study together in the afternoons, study until Caitie knew fifth-grade math and science inside out, until Caitie, too, was dreaming about fractions. Caitie hadn't let Hannah give up. Hannah wouldn't let Caitie give up, either.

Clutching Judith in one arm and feeling more grown up than she had ever felt in her life, Hannah ran downstairs to call Caitie.

25

It was hot. Already in the low eighties at ten o'clock in the morning, the temperature was predicted to soar to the mid-nineties by afternoon, near the record for early June. Mrs. McCloskey looked hot. Her blue blouse had turned purple under the arms from perspiration, and damp tendrils of hair straggled untidily from her bun.

"Good morning, boys and girls," she said. "I have some good news for you today."

For a fleeting moment Hannah hoped the news would be that at last they were going to begin a real art project. Mrs. McCloskey had finally stopped assigning Clorox-bottle projects a few weeks ago, but she had turned right away to projects involving cardboard egg cartons.

"The superintendent of schools has announced the winners for the countywide art contest. It's my pleasure to tell you that one of our members has won a ribbon—first prize, no less, out of all the elementary schools in the county."

Hannah stared down at her desk. Someone who had sat there before her had carved initials into the wood: H.T. + S.L. Who were H.T. and S.L.? What had become of them?

"I think we should all give her a hand: Hannah Keddie!"

"Hannah!" Caitie jumped out of her seat and hugged her. The others clapped and whistled. Hannah felt a ridiculous, happy grin slowly spreading across her face. Maybe *The New Yorker* magazine was right. Maybe she *was* a talented artist. Maybe someday, if she worked very hard, she *would* have pictures on the covers of magazines and in art museums.

As Mrs. McCloskey passed out the egg cartons for the day's assignment—an egg-carton mobile—she paused respectfully at Hannah's desk. "I don't think you need to do our next project," she said. "Why don't you use the time to draw or paint—whatever you'd like."

For the rest of the class period, Mrs. McCloskey tiptoed past Hannah so as not to disturb the great artist's concentration. It was embarrassing to be treated all of a sudden like a young Michelangelo, but pleasant, too.

When the bell rang for lunch, Hannah and Caitie walked together to the library. Mrs. Tomacki had agreed to let them bring their books there and study while they ate.

That day Mrs. Tomacki greeted Hannah with a hug and a smile. "I heard about the contest," she said. "Hooray for our side! We'll have to plan a party to celebrate. Right, Caitie?"

"After the next math test," Caitie said with a groan.

The girls settled themselves at a table next to the window and took out their math textbooks. "So *that's* what a least common denominator is," Hannah remembered Caitie saying a couple of days ago. "If I had known *that* was what it was, I'd have done a lot better on those dumb assignments."

They worked through a chapter's worth of problems, then Caitie put her pencil down. "Maybe I won't be a model, after all. Maybe I'll be a mathematician."

Hannah stared at her in disbelief.

"Just kidding," Caitie said. Hannah laughed weakly. "But it's not so bad, studying, when you really do it. I think sometimes I used to goof off just to get at my parents. You know, because they were gone so much? Kind of so they'd notice me."

"But you don't want to do it anymore?"

"Well, it's not that I don't still get mad at them," Caitie said. "But I'm the one who might have to repeat fifth grade, not them."

"Speaking of which—" Hannah said.

Caitie picked up her pencil with a sigh. "Okay. Show me again how to multiply fractions."

After school the girls descended on Caitie's air-conditioned rec room. Rita brought them tall glasses of ice-cold root beer with scoops of vanilla ice cream floating on top. They needed all the refreshments they could get, because they were hard at work on another play for Sam. Sam was still in love, but not with Roger. Evan Dixon had kissed her on the lips late in the spin-the-bottle game at Caitie's party, and at that moment Sam had realized that she wasn't in love with Roger and never had been—not *really* in love, not in *love* in love, the way she was with Evan. The purpose of the new play was to give Evan the idea of asking Sam to go steady with him. They had started it a few days ago. So far it went like this:

THE PERILS OF SAMANTHA METCALF

ACT II

The curtain rises on a typical cafeteria scene. At one table Brian Taylor, Michael Malone, Justin Seavey, and Evan Dixon are eating their lunches. They are laughing and dropping ice cubes down one another's collars. At the next table Samantha Metcalf, Dawn Klein, Caitie Crystal, and Hannah Keddie are eating their lunches. They speak loudly enough to be overheard by the boys.

CAITIE: Did you know that my cousin Bonnie went steady six times when she was in seventh grade?

DAWN: My cousin Diana went steady three times in *sixth* grade.

CAITIE: Bonnie went steady once in *fifth* grade. It was toward the end of the year. In June, I think.

SAM: June is a good time of year to go steady.

CAITIE: Can you believe there were boys in her fifth-grade class grown-up enough to ask a girl to go steady with them?

DAWN: The boys in *our* class are all babies.

CAITIE: Especially Brian.

SAM: No, they're not.

DAWN: Name one that isn't.

SAM [*Shyly*]:   Well, Evan . . .

Hannah hadn't let Caitie write in any lines for her to speak. She couldn't very well make the Hannah character say, "Growing up has nothing to do with going steady. Nothing at all!" But she thought it, anyway.

All the same, it was fun being at Caitie's, sipping a root-beer float and listening to the funny dialogue

Caitie invented. Hannah didn't have to go along with everything the other girls did. She could still be Hannah, different from the others, but liking them, too.

She had been afraid everyone would make fun of her after Caitie's party, but, aside from a couple of snide remarks from Dawn, no one had. Dawn would never like her, but that was okay. Even Caitie didn't really like Dawn, and Caitie liked almost everybody.

Most of all Hannah had dreaded facing Michael, but he had been waiting for her at the bus the Monday after the party.

"Listen," he had said. "About Saturday night. I'm sorry if I upset you. I just thought—"

"It was my fault," Hannah had stopped him. "It was just—I don't know—I guess I don't like games like that."

"It was pretty dumb," he'd agreed. "So we're still friends?"

Hannah had nodded, relieved beyond measure.

They finished the play by four-thirty and the others left soon after, but Hannah stayed on, waiting for a ride from her father. She was always happiest when she and Caitie were by themselves. They had started their own special, top-secret project together, too: making doll clothes for the poor Barbies who had come to the tea party in fabric scraps. Hannah liked to sew, and she was teaching Caitie.

"Should I get a second set of ear holes pierced, or

not?" Caitie asked now, studying herself in her vanity mirror.

"Not," Hannah answered promptly. She leaned forward to see her own reflection. "Are my bangs getting too long? Is it time to get my hair cut again?"

"Well, I was thinking it needed a trim, but I wasn't going to say anything. I figured you were growing it back long, and I didn't want it to be like I was trying to make you over again, or anything."

"I've decided that I like it short," Hannah said. "Now that I'm used to it, I really do. Right now I like everything, every single thing in the whole world."

"You know, Hannah," Caitie said, flinging herself back onto the bed, "I'm glad I flunked out of the Waverly School, because if I hadn't I wouldn't have gone to Greenwood Park, and if I hadn't gone to Greenwood Park, you and I wouldn't be friends. Let's be friends forever, okay? Even when we're really truly grown up, with jobs and husbands and babies and everything."

"Even when we're really truly grown up," Hannah promised, "we'll still be friends."